# YOU DIDN'T GET THIS FROM ME

## A Novel of Media and Politics

### MIKE VIQUEIRA

ISBN: 1540791750
ISBN 13: 9781540791757
Library of Congress Control Number: 2016920312
CreateSpace Independent Publishing Platform
North Charleston, South Carolina

*For Kim. Thank you for your patience, and for your faith in me.*

# Chapter 1

They say that power is an aphrodisiac. But who falls under its spell? The people near the powerful or the powerful themselves?

One afternoon in the spring of 2013, Loretta Jean Polk stood amid a fawning herd of paunchy old bulls, a glimmering jewel whose radiance illuminated the smoky air of the Speaker's ceremonial reception chamber, rendering her in a soft focus suitable for either a silent film star or an aging television news personality.

She wore what appeared to be a majorette's uniform: red-sequined boy shorts with a matching tuxedo-tail jacket accented in black lapels and cuffs. Beneath was a fitted vest that served as a kind of corset, cinched at the waist and gently widening at each of five ascending gold buttons until it reached its apex, a point just shy of scandalous and dipping toward inappropriate, revealing the cleavage between two stout, ponderous bosoms. She stood regally atop black stiletto-heeled mules on tiny feet that flowed upward into legs ten yards long—athletic, but not too muscular in tone—tan and unblemished.

Her nose was strong and sensually assertive. Thick eyebrows conjured thoughts of Sophia Loren, circa 1965. A riot of streaked, glossy curls erupted from her head and cascaded past her shoulders. She was a crystal tulip glass filled with the finest champagne, a frothy elixir in a suspenseful rise to the brim.

"What an unbelievable piece of ass," observed Billy O'Nesti as he watched from behind a false wall of the chamber.

"I can't get past the hat," replied his friend Tom Salta, chief congressional correspondent for the American Broadcasting Network. The only thing marring this divine apparition was the giant foam hat in the shape of a soup spoon that tenuously balanced on her head. "It's really getting in my way."

"I think it completes the look rather nicely." O'Nesti was a congressional producer for BOP, one of the cable TV news outfits. He and Tom were kindred spirits who hung out a lot killing time, waiting for news to happen, and clinging to the same dry sense of fatalism that was their last defense against the insanity of covering the US House, a place where anything goes and no one gives a damn.

Every Wednesday afternoon they sneaked into a tack room near the old horse stables, up a ladder and through a forgotten crawl space, and then down into a three-foot gap between the original Aquia stone lining the chamber and the drywall erected to improve acoustics at press conferences. A mural depicting the Constitutional Convention of 1787 had been painted directly onto the wallboard, and the two journalists peered through a crack in James Madison's forehead into the weekly meeting of the semisecret Chowder and Marching Society. Today Congresswoman Polk was being inducted as its newest—and first female—member.

Protocol compelled new members of the society to wear the ceremonial uniform. That usually involved dragging out the same threadbare drum major's costume that had been salvaged from someone's attic years ago, tossing it at the unfortunate aspirant, and then howling with derision as he emerged from a dressing room looking like a homeless deserter from the Pope's Swiss Guard.

That wouldn't do for someone like Loretta Jean, who hadn't come this far in life without understanding the importance of making a positive impression. She'd had something a bit more flattering assembled for the occasion, and when she swept into the room the only howling was in the sclerotic hearts of the men who now competed for her attentions.

The most important part of the ceremony was the "crowning" of a new member with the Spoon Hat, the solemn moment when a Chowderhead was born. The ritual had the attribute of humiliation—essential to a proper hazing—without the effort involved in something more proactive like a paddle wheel, though considering today's inductee, there would have been no shortage of volunteers.

"Loretta Jean Polk. Tell me everything you know about her," Tom said to O'Nesti. It was a game of theirs to quiz each other on the biographies of members of Congress.

"That's not much of a challenge, but here goes," replied Billy. He put one hand up to his ear and affected a Winchellesque squawk. "Beginning life amid humble origins on the high plains of Wyoming, Loretta Jean Tisher began her political rise as an eager young assistant in the 2004 Senate campaign of William Polk, the stalwart House conservative bidding for election to the upper chamber. Polk lost his bid, but won the girl when the long hours the two spent traveling together on the lonesome Wyoming campaign trail yielded a May-September romance."

"How scintillating!" Tom said sarcastically, and then pretended to read from his phone. "Let's go to our Twitter feed. Here's a poster from Casper who wants to know, 'Wasn't Congressman Polk already married at the time?'"

"Polk, the legendary chairman of the Commerce and Finance Committee, left his wife of thirty years to take up with the big-tittied Tisher, a woman thirty-five years his junior. They were wed the following spring," Billy solemnly reported. "Facing Wyoming voters once more the next fall, Polk reclaimed his old

House seat, prevailing despite attacks on his personal conduct launched by his opponent, a popular television anchorman who led in the polls before it was revealed that he was actually a citizen of Belize."

"So it's a story of redemption!" Tom brought his hands together at his heart. "Oh, there simply must be a happy ending. Please, please tell me that there is a happy ending."

"So there is, dear listener," Billy continued. "Shortly after taking the oath of office that January, Polk and his new wife joined colleagues and their spouses on a congressional fact-finding delegation to Molokai, where Polk died scuba diving under fifty feet of water while investigating the effects of El Niño on aquatic life. Happily, Mrs. Polk escaped unharmed."

"It's so wonderful that Loretta Jean was safe," said Tom.

"Safe as houses, one might say, for it seems that at the behest of state party elders, the grieving Widow Polk returned to Wyoming and ran for and won the special election to replace her dearly departed husband here in your US House of Reprehensibles. Sympathetic leaders then broke with precedent and granted her the seniority accrued to her husband, with all the perks accorded thereto, including his coveted seat on Commerce and Finance," Billy recounted as he wrapped the story. "And then a monster came and ate everyone." His performance thus concluded, Billy lowered his hand from his ear and bowed deeply.

"A stirring tale—brilliantly rendered, I might add—that epitomizes the grit and determination that made this great country a beacon of freedom around the world," Tom said.

Inside, Loretta Jean was all smiles, only too glad to endure the ogling of the decrepit trolls now surrounding her. It was a small price to pay for the opportunity to break the Chowderhead gender barrier and enter this ridiculous fraternity, an upper echelon of backroom Washington power. Since the death of her husband and her election nine years ago, Polk had demonstrated time and again that she was no ingénue. It quickly became apparent that she had all the hallmarks of the Washington success story: relentless ambition, minimal need for sleep, and an ear for politics that rivaled most of the seasoned pros that had been at it for decades. She was a beautiful woman who understood there was something in the nature of power—something physiological—that triggered in these men a belief that they were as desirable as the silverback in a troupe of lowland gorillas.

In point of fact, few possessed that kind of animal magnetism, but to see Loretta was to understand that they would be beating their chests over her whenever she was within their domain. Loretta could redirect their lust for her into a positive force for self-advancement, to contort their ardor as if she were a master of jujitsu. A score of men perpetually believed that they were at last on the verge of having her when in reality they had no shot. But they would keep trying, lavishing her with adulation, telling her secrets in the hopes of gaining her confidence only to have her employ their information to her own advantage. It was the psychological nature of the powerful man to be free of self-doubt, to never pause for a moment of introspection that might allow him to see what a fool he had made of himself. It always amused her to find a potbellied, seventy-five-year-old subcommittee chairman with a gold wedding band and yellowed dentures who didn't have a moment's hesitation in hitting on her. In the end, her skill in managing their tumescence was a key to her success. Because she let them keep their dignity, they all still thought they would get their chance.

"I feel like I'm watching a nature documentary on the hypersexuality of goats," Tom marveled.

Loretta gracefully spun from the grasp of a silver-maned appropriator who had slipped one hand around her waist while holding a whiskey sour in the other.

"Look at how hard my boy is going for it out there," Billy said of the committee warlord who kept finding a reason to place his hands on Loretta during the course of conversation. "If it were anyone but her, I'd say that she was going to pop him at any minute."

"This must be chronicled," Tom declared. He raised his cellphone and aligned the lens against the crack in the wall.

There was a commotion on the far side of the room. "Here comes Mr. Big," Billy said as people jostled for position between the door and Loretta Polk, hoping for some significant eye contact or a quick word with Majority Leader Zach Dickey, who was now entering the chamber to huzzahs.

"And he's just in time to save our damsel in distress." Tom and Billy stood bent at the waist and temple to temple, peeping.

Loretta and her coterie of sycophants—including the white-haired letch who a moment before appeared ready to dry hump her leg—now stepped back and joined the others in hailing the leader. They knew that Dickey would be making his way in the direction of today's honoree. They knew this because of another thing they thought they knew, which, depending on the rumor du jour, was that Loretta and Dickey were either lovers or future running mates. Or both. Not that anyone was there to gossip, mind you. But just so, maybe it was a good idea for the Chowderheads to kiss Dickey's ring as he passed by on his way to greet the fabulous Loretta Jean Polk.

Members lined up to buttonhole their leader. "If I vote with you on the free trade bill, will you get me on Ways and Means?"… "Those sunzabitches on Appropriations want to delete my bridge project! I told them I had your commitment"…"Have you given any thought to my request to speak at my son's graduation?"… "Can I use your Redskins tickets next Monday night?" The list was as long as it was petty. Dickey managed to affect a look of concern where warranted, to nod his head knowingly when understanding was called for, to offer a shoulder to cry on when sympathy was in order, or to share outrage at the terrible injustice of it all. His body man and loyal aide, Stu Albertson, stayed at his elbow taking careful notes of every commitment, like a scribe at medieval court. It was a perfect illustration of Dickey's cardinal rule of politics: always keep your constituents happy. And as these guys were the ones who elected Dickey to leader, they were his most important constituency. His great skill was to simply have the patience and discipline to let them talk until they were all punched out and forgot what they were bitching about in the first place.

"Politics is war without the bullets," he always told Stu. "Let the passions of the day be funneled through Washington, where your dedicated public servants could be trusted to fight it out against the forces that were taking this country to hell in a hand-basket. We'll take to the floor of the House or call a hearing and yell and scream as if our very beings were possessed of your collective outrage and save you the trouble of fighting it out in the streets to settle your differences. And if when we finish channeling your anger you still want something done, then we just might actually pass a law." The way Dickey saw it, hot air was an undervalued commodity.

"I am so sick of this guy's song and dance I could scream," Billy declared.

"He's heinous, no question about it," agreed Tom. "But in a way I admire him for the way he plays the game."

Billy stepped back from the peephole and turned to Tom with an incredulous look. "Excuse me? The echo off the stone back here is playing tricks with my ears. I thought I just heard you defend the Antichrist."

"Well, I mean it's true that he's the prince of phonies; I'm not going to stand here and argue that. But look at the effort the guy puts into politicking each and every one of these guys. You've got to give him some credit for doing the spadework, anyway."

Billy rolled his eyes. "You look out there and then with a straight face tell me you see a sincere politician with the nation's best interests at heart and not a guy who makes Machiavelli look like a do-gooder," Billy said.

"Oh for chrissakes, don't act like I'm a heretic. I didn't say I liked his politics," Tom said. He didn't want to fight with Billy, his best buddy.

Too late.

"It's about integrity! It has nothing to do with politics!" Billy declared. He had that wounded look. "The fact that you would even imply that I could give half a shit about his politics I take as a personal insult. I'm a goddamn professional journalist!" He reached for his wallet and produced a voter registration card and held it up close to Tom's face. "A fucking registered Independent, OK? An objective observer. I can't believe I'm hearing this from you of all people."

"Whoa there. What is that supposed to mean?" Now Tom was hurt. "Look, I'm sorry if you took me to mean that you're not the living embodiment of Edward R. Fucking Murrow. But I think you need to ask yourself if our fanatical hatred of Dickey is about high-minded ideals of public service or about the fact that every time we look at the guy we're reminded of how irrelevant our lives have become."

"Oh, please. Spare me the navel-gazing."

"Come on, Billy. Look at us! The highlight of our week is this glorified peep show. Last week I pitched a story about the tort reform bill to the network and they laughed in my face. If we aren't chasing some congressman around who may or may not be banging an intern, then we're nowhere. This beat is reduced to the status of some twisted cult."

"Fine. You don't have to tell me all that. I've been in this business since BC, baby, Before Cable. I'm here to tell you that it's a different world now. Maybe you're just pissed because I'm getting stories on the air and you're not, and you can't handle that."

Tom stifled the urge to laugh out loud. That was rich coming from Billy, he thought. Somewhere inside of him the network snob still clung to life, wistful for the good old days. Tom knew that Billy secretly hated the fact that he ended up at an outfit like BOP, where on a typical afternoon the nationwide viewing audience might not be enough to fill RFK stadium.

"As if anybody is watching cable," Tom jabbed.

"Oh, I see." Billy was livid. "Now we're getting somewhere. You are obviously superior to me, seeing as how you work for the big bad dinosaur network. Is that what this is about? Well, allow me to make a prediction. Within twelve months of us standing here having this discussion, you will be in my bureau chief's office begging for a job after your network has become so irrelevant that not even Zach Dickey would pause to give you the time of day! You'll end up a ranting blogger with a podcast!"

Tom saw where this was going, but he couldn't help himself. "OK, fine. If that's the case, then tell me why Dickey is going out of his way to fill me in on a scandal involving none other than *her*," Tom said, gesturing to where Loretta stood on the other side of the drywall. "It's going to blow your ass right out of the water."

Billy froze, leaning forward midrant, mouth agape. Tom watched as confusion, anger, hurt, and then jealousy played across his friend's face, all compressed into a ten-second time lapse, ending with a smirk. "Let's have it then, old buddy," Billy said. "Let's let that cat out of its bag."

They had a pact. Mutually assured destruction. If one had something good, he had to share with the other. But this story was different, bigger by a factor of infinity than anything they had shared in the past.

"I cannot give it to you, man."

"You're going to leave me hanging? Come on, man! Did I or did I not share that memo on the tax cut package last month? Have you forgotten that? I fished that out of the committee room trash can myself."

"I could hardly read it for all the coffee stains and shit, but true enough," Tom said, chuckling. "But I'm talking about something much bigger. Much. You have to promise me, and I mean swear on the God of Political Independents or whatever god you pray to, that you will not say a word, make a phone call, wink, nod, or otherwise move a muscle on this story until I can get it on the air."

"Done."

"You swear?" Tom pressed.

"On everything that is holy."

A dubious oath, coming from Billy, but good enough for Tom. He trusted his wingman like a brother.

# Chapter 2

*The demagogue is one who preaches doctrines he knows
to be untrue to men he knows to be idiots.*

—H. L. Mencken

As the two friends stood in the cramped crawlspace, Tom began
to tell Billy the bizarre tale of his encounter with Dickey, and
how the majority leader gave him a lead on the story of a lifetime.

It happened just the day before Loretta's debut at Chowder
and Marching—at Dickey's weekly media briefing. The session
was held in an ornate foyer adjacent to Dickey's suite of offices in the Capitol, a stuffy space of dark paneling and pilasters.
One of the several original Gilbert Stuart portraits of George
Washington hung on the wall in a place of privilege, providing
both a camera backdrop and a silent context of legitimacy to
what was usually a farce.

The majority leader entered the room and took his place at the podium. A squad of twenty or so Capitol reporters was anxiously arrayed before him like infantry mustered for a charge, the cameras lined up at their backs like artillery deployed to support their advance. In the eternal triumph of hope over experience, the gathered press was ready for Dickey to say something of substance and make news. Tom knew better. He stood apart from the scrum, disinterested and loitering in the back of the room.

"The promise of salvation is the essential hope of the Judeo-Christian tradition, and the condemned have a right to bask in that tradition, regardless of religious affiliation," Dickey intoned at the start, revealing his proposal to require the Bureau of Prisons to post the twenty-third psalm on death rows across the land. "The right to spiritual renewal is God given, a gift that should be available to all Americans."

As a network correspondent on Capitol Hill, Tom trafficked in bullshit. He was a connoisseur and a wholesaler. He hated that he had to listen to Dickey. But it was his job. He hated his job.

The first lie of the politician is telling voters the things they *want* to believe about themselves, leveraging the space between what we imagine we are—a self-made success owing to our innate virtue, ability, and work ethic—and what we actually are.

The second lie is telling voters the things they're *willing* to believe about the opposition. Confirming their worst suspicions about The Other. Animating delusions. Demonizing the enemy and turning him into a cartoon villain who must be crushed at all costs. Scratching the primordial itch to choose up sides and fight. Political rhetoric has never been about sweet reason. The best politicians, the survivors, understand this. The hacks do not.

Majority Leader Dickey was not a hack.

"Yea, though I walk through the valley of death, I will fear no evil..." Dickey's eyes were tightly shut and his chin raised heavenward.

Tom wasn't listening. He was watching a fetid stream of figures and stock quotes flow like an open sewer through his smart phone. Figures that, with each passing day, had chronicled the collapse of his stock portfolio and foretold his impending financial destruction. It was breaking news for his bank account.

He was too angry to pay attention to Dickey. The parent company of Tom's network, Minton Systems, was on a very bad run. It seemed every new financial story was shot through with doom-and-gloom quotes from analysts who said the market cap was still way too high and that the company's debt strategy was sure to lead to ruin. Could be the largest corporate disaster in American history, said the guy on the financial news network. The stock price was plummeting. Now there were rumors of malfeasance and a congressional investigation.

"Thy rod and thy staff, they comfort me…"

Tom had listened to all the old-timers at the American Broadcasting Network who were around when Minton Systems bought the company twenty years ago, the ones who had found riches just by lasting long enough to watch their old shares of ABN go through the roof. Most of them were living large by now, driving sixties vintage English sports cars to their Bethany Beach houses. *Don't be a fool,* they counseled. *Forget those boring, safe, old mutual funds. This baby is a rock. An index fund? Don't make us laugh.*

It all made sense to Tom, so all of his 401(k) contributions went into Minton, the company match on top of it. If he had a few thousand lying about, well then, he would throw that into the pot as well. That was four years ago. Tom had spent those years kicking in the max, and at top price. Now the financial experts were calling for Minton to spin off ABN in an effort to streamline and follow the business-school axiom of *stick to your knitting.* The last four months were spent riding a runaway pony all the way down to the water. The only question now was would it stop there…or go all the way under?

Tom was lost in his anger and forgot where he was. "God DAMNIT!" he yelled out loud.

Cameramen backed away from their viewfinders and reporters looked up from their notepads, their ennui shattered. Dickey's eyes refocused on the here and now, like a snake handler shaken from a trance. He was the kind of guy whose biggest shame in life was the time his daughter got kicked out of Baylor for dancing. The man was a paragon of Southern piety. Someone coughed.

"Everything OK back there, Tom?" Dickey's tone was somewhere between fake concern and genuine anger.

Tom saw his career flash before his eyes. Two years as a desk assistant and nine years climbing the on-air ladder from Framingham to Fargo, finally going national on ABN, and then getting to Washington. Now one little shouted blasphemy and a phone call from this hard-on to Tom's bureau chief meant he was back to market number 103. *Good Morning, Fort Wayne!*

"Beg your pardon, Mr. Leader." Tourette's? Early-onset dementia? Tom's instinct was to go for the pity angle.

Then he remembered that no one cared.

Fifteen years ago the title of chief congressional correspondent at ABN would have been fraught with prestige. Now, Tom might as well have told people he was a GS-12 at the Department of Commerce. His producers hardly bothered to read his pitches. If they didn't care about a $600 billion defense bill, they wouldn't care about a profane outburst. They were more prone to distrust someone who didn't curse.

Up in front of the cameras Dickey was back at it. "And so I have spoken with the committee chairman, and he has agreed to consider this matter with the utmost alacrity."

Zach Dickey had the demagogue's intuitive feel for pushing voters' buttons. He understood that voters could be angry or they could be apathetic. There were no in-betweens. So he played to their dread and anxiety over the bewildering changes in the world around them, stoking their resentment at being told that the standards of behavior they had thought were long settled they now had to reform. And for what? Some abstract ideal that required them to get out of their comfort zone in order to defend against a threat they couldn't see, touch, or feel. Dickey could frame every issue as a moral question, cloak it in ideology, and apply his one-size-fits-all template to complicated questions, about which most people were completely ignorant. The trick was to proclaim change itself as a threat to the moral order, and then reverse engineer the rhetoric to fit the conclusion. Dickey was a master practitioner at the top of his game.

As Dickey went on speaking, Tom borrowed a pen and began a pantomime of note taking. What he was actually doing was tabulating the damage wrought by this dog of a company he worked for: $10,000 in the hole over the last month alone.

# CHAPTER 3

After a very perfunctory period of questions and answers, Dickey had stopped yakking and vanished. Newspaper reporters cast eyes sideways at Tom, wondering what in the hell was wrong with the TV guy. Tom avoided them.

Tom turned to find Stu Albertson, Dickey's aide-de-camp, hovering just inches away.

"Look, Stu, I know what you're going to say, and I'm sorry if I detracted from the decorum befitting this very important event, but I really wasn't directing it at Dickey." Tom couldn't resist a little smart mouth with the staff, even now.

"Don't worry about it. I know just how you feel," said Stu, typically. He was the yes-man prototype, always trailing a step behind a powerful chairman and struggling with a fat accordion binder—pasty face befitting a man who spent every hour overshadowed by his boss and a musty wardrobe that uncannily matched the wallpaper of every room in the Capitol. He had been with Dickey since Dickey's days as a talk-radio host back in Tennessee, producing the drive-time show (The Need for Screed) that launched his career. Stu was a political caddy, calculating the yardage on every issue and selecting the proper club for his boss, who always hit the green in regulation. It was enough for him to be in proximity to power. He never aspired to actually have any. He was Radar O'Reilly with an oak desk and all the charisma of a pile of soggy used tires.

"Actually, Tom," Stu continued, "the boss was wondering if we could all sit down for a little chat in his office. Do you have a second? He has something that he thinks you might find very useful." He placed a clammy hand on Tom's shoulder.

"Don't tell me—it's something so juicy that it just has to be off the record. Am I right?" Once in a while a member would make a pretense of taking Tom into his confidence, maybe invite him into his historic hideaway office—the asymmetrical warrens in the corners of the building—for that extraspecial ambience of exclusivity. The personal touch. A senator might produce a bottle of scotch, pour a couple of fingers for both of them, then move to the window and grandly sweep his arm across the vista of the National Mall like he was Erich von Stroheim and they were gentlemanly adversaries in *The Grand Illusion*. The information they shared was almost always self-serving crap.

But having nothing better to do, Tom agreed.

"Tom! Come on in!" Dickey came at him with a meaty paw, the heels of his Western boots thudding into the carpet of his office. He swatted at the makeup bib that flapped up over his face as he approached. "Do you think this twenty-third psalm thing is going to play for you tonight?"

"Are you serious?" Tom said with too much edge.

"I'm not, so relax, will you for heaven's sake, Tom?" Dickey drawled. His free hand gripped Tom's elbow. "I worry about you, Tom, I really do," he said. "You've gotten yourself so wound up that now you're shouting out swears to the wind! You do a heck of a job, son, but once in a while you've got to stop and smell the lilacs!"

Dickey let go of Tom and sat before a mirror propped against the wall. Without a word, Stu moved to his side and, picking up a makeup sponge, began smearing another layer of foundation onto Dickey's jowls.

"Got to freshen up for the next event!" Dickey's reflected stare bore in on Tom as his head rocked back and forth with the force of Stu's methodical application. "I've got a little proposition for you, Tom, and I would appreciate it if we could go off the record for a moment."

Tom sighed theatrically and nodded.

"If it makes you feel any better, we're all as sick of this chicken shit as you are," Dickey said. Tom noted the use of profanity. Very simpatico.

"In case you haven't heard, I'm thinking about making my move next year. Being ignored by your network isn't exactly helping with my name recognition."

Dickey wanted to be president of the United States.

"Yes, I've heard. And, with due respect, it's not your name recognition that you have to worry about. Your problem is that everyone outside your loyal cadre of Kool-Aid drinkers thinks you're an asshole," Tom sneered, then added, "sir."

The leader glanced at Stu, who, for the first time in Tom's memory, was getting some color in his cheeks.

"No offense to you personally, Stu, of course," said Tom.

Dickey took it all in stride. To his way of thinking, Tom Salta wasn't worth the effort it took to be angry. He was just another one of the coastal pansy elite, who were, at their essence, more intolerant than the conservatives they sneered at. Salta and the rest of them would be better journalists if they stopped for half a second to think about why actual voters out there in flyover country thought people like Salta were the real assholes.

Dickey wasn't concerned with moral distinctions. Who's right, who's wrong, he marveled at how everyone in Washington wasted time trying to win first prize in the debating society. Fact checking—ha! Real people weren't concerned with someone else's idea of the facts. In the end, what did it get them? A good argument was useful to Dickey. But only as a means of distracting folks from the unsightly process of making the political sausage. Arguing with reporters was a loser's game, if for no other reason than they always got the last word. If you pissed them off badly enough—and this usually involved leaking something sexy to a competitor—they would go out of their way to find a means to screw you. The more skilled among them could publicly slip in the knife, twist it a few times, yank it back out dripping blood and tissue, and still claim objectivity. One local Tennessee reporter never failed to mention Dickey's age in his copy. "Dickey, 70, of Bartlett, said today that he will do everything in his power to see that the new road is built." The reporter knew full well that the majority leader, a man who dyed his eyebrows and spent $100 a month on age-defying facial serum, lost another hair on his head every time he saw his age in print.

Dickey chose the existential view. Reporters owed him nothing. And if their only concern was their own preservation and prosperity, then that was just one more thing they had in common with the politicians they covered. Both sides could benefit from a little mutual exploitation. Which brought his mind back to why he was sitting here talking to this sniveling prick to begin with.

"Before you start screaming again like one of these homeless out on DuPont Circle, Tom, I think that you had better hear us out. We're talking about something that is a guaranteed scoop. Do y'all still use that word?" He turned to Stu, who nodded in solemn affirmation. "I imagine you'll be appreciative. That is, if you still have any interest in actually getting somewhere in this town," said Dickey, twisting a knife of his own.

"Sir, this being the United States Congress, and you being the majority leader, I'd say that you could probably leak things that would bring me to journalistic ecstasy," Tom said. "But experience tells me what you're peddling is just another tease."

"Are we off the record, Tom, or aren't we?" Dickey glanced again at Stu. He was having second thoughts about this whole idea. They had agreed that Salta was the perfect candidate. But he was clearly reckless.

"Sure. Why not?" said Tom.

"Let me speak hypothetically here for a moment, Tom," Dickey began. "Suppose that a certain member of Congress was sitting on a very powerful committee, and that committee was in the middle of an investigation that provided lots of very inside information—very sensitive stuff that is potentially very lucrative—on a certain very big company. And let's say that this member is using this information to enrich him-or-herself in a manner that is most definitely unethical and almost assuredly illegal. All it would take would be for a talented young buck like this fella standing here before me to do a little basic reporting, and all hell would break loose. Now, would you say that's something these mysterious people who produce your news programs would think is a story?"

"I would say that sounds like a story that would quite possibly win me a prestigious award," Tom said. "But before I rush out to get my tux cleaned, let me go ahead and admit that I'm a little skeptical."

"Of course you are, Tom! Of course you are. It's like my ol' daddy used to say: If it sounds too good to be true, then it usually is!" Dickey's use of aw-shucks idioms rose in inverse proportion to his comfort level. "You being a reporter and all, it's perfectly natural that you would have some questions."

"I'm glad you understand. So let's begin with some basics. Are you simply passing along some cloakroom scuttlebutt about a member of the other party? Because I can get gossip about the other guys by simply walking in circles around the rotunda."

"What I am passing along is a hypothetical, first of all." Dickey kept a fig leaf handy until he was sure Salta would play ball. "But no, this hypothetical member of Congress would be a member of my own party."

Tom's long-dormant reporter's instincts were suddenly kicking in. "Let's stop talking in code. Who is it?"

"Take it easy there, boy!" Dickey said. He saw that the greater Tom's enthusiasm, the stronger his hand. "Assuming that we are talking about an actual, bona fide set of circumstances, we're going to have to come to a business agreement here before we really get to telling stories out of school."

There was a price, of course. Tom didn't mind. If it were even close to the truth, Tom was going to lead the evening broadcast for a week and more. He'd be the toast of the Radio and Television Gallery. The information would likely have come from the fifth column of loyal ex-staffers Dickey had strategically placed in virtually every committee, lobby shop, or political operation of any consequence on the Hill or K Street. The Dickey Diaspora was run like a crime syndicate, complete with whispering informants and strong-armed shakedowns for anyone who stood in the way of the expansion of his political influence. Dickey and Stu knew things that could make or break the careers of half the people on the Hill.

"I'm having a hard time seeing what I can do for you in return, Mr. Leader. You might think that I'd sell my soul for a good tip, and you could be right. But I still can't get your death row idea on the air."

Dickey waved his hand disdainfully, knocking the makeup sponge from Stu's hand. "I'm not talking about that cockamamie death row nonsense."

Tom's mind scanned the universe of favors that he could possibly provide Dickey. "I'm not going to kill anyone for you, Mr. Leader."

"Well I'm certainly glad to hear that, Tom." Dickey chuckled through his inscrutable smile.

"OK. Let's take this from the top. You have information that we both know I want badly; I'm not going to pretend otherwise. There is absolutely nothing in the history of how you operate that would lead me to believe that this information is going to be free of charge."

Dickey nodded. "Tom, it's like the man said: information is power. That's always been a part of my credo."

"Right. Thank you, Confucius. Now I'm going to ask you straight up: What's your price?"

Dickey liked seeing Salta squirm. He couldn't understand how these reporters got through each day with an allegiance to nothing and no one. There was no ideology, no credo to guide their behavior and, more to the point, what they reported to folks.

Dickey always hated it when he heard people say that politics was a put-on, Kabuki theater, and at the end of the day all of the wrangling amounted to nothing. He had a different interpretation: the void was at the core of the people charged with deciding what was reported on the news. They called it "objectivity"—as if it having no beliefs were a belief in and of itself. To Dickey a better term would have been "emptiness." A guy like Salta would cloak himself in principle to hide his cowardice.

"You know what I think, Tom? I think you think too much. Either that or you give me way too much credit as a conspirator. Hell, if I were half the plotter y'all say I am, I'd have managed to get elected king by now," said Dickey. "The truth of the matter is that I have no price. You were wrong a second ago when you said that about me. I'm always willing to help people who can use my help, it's a Volunteer tradition. I'm empowering you for free," he said grandly. "No charge, my friend."

"So you're an altruist. Who knew?"

Dickey scowled. "One thing you seem to be missing is the fact that there is a member of Congress who is not only conducting themselves in a manner not befitting the trust of the American public, but is also bringing shame to the party that I love," said Dickey, fronting righteousness. "Why would you think I would aid and abet this kind of behavior by remaining silent? You see, there is in fact something in it for me. I would like to see this institution purged of this insidious germ. And you know what they say, Tom. Sometimes sunshine is the best disinfectant."

Tom was puzzled. When someone sees a crime being committed, they call the police. Or, if the suspect is a member of Congress, maybe the ethics committee. They don't call the press, at least not a guy like Dickey. Either way, it really didn't matter much to Tom. In a way it was better that he didn't know. "What about that business transaction you mentioned?" Tom asked.

Dickey's smile collapsed into leathery, variegated folds, an east Tennessee landscape from thirty thousand feet. "The business of trust, Tom. That's what I'm talking about. Not horse trading. Not logrolling. Trust."

"Trust." Tom repeated the word dully. Whatever Dickey's angle was, he was playing it for all it was worth, he thought.

"Trust is the coin of the realm around these parts, Tom," Dickey continued. "Now, I know that you know that. There may come a time in this story when the heat is going to come down on you pretty strong. All I'm asking is that you keep your sources confidential, like the good reporter that I know you are."

That confirmed it for Tom. He was being used. He didn't care.

"You have my word," Tom replied. "Now, who is this corrupted member who has affronted you so?"

Dickey was silent. Instead it was Stu who spoke from his spot in the corner.

"Loretta Jean Polk," he said.

# Chapter 4

*One of the penalties of refusing to participate in politics*
*is that you end up being governed by your inferiors.*

—*Plato*

So that was the backstory, the tale Tom told to his friend Billy as they stood hidden in the crawl space at Chowder and Marching. When Tom wrapped it up, Billy paused for a glassy-eyed moment, and when he came back from a place in the depths of credulity, he raised himself up once more to peer through the hole in the wall.

"I wonder what she can do for an orange prison jumpsuit," he wondered aloud.

Inside the room Loretta's Styrofoam hat bobbed along in the current of humanity swirling toward the majority leader, whose head, thanks to the generous heels of his boots, was the only other object visible on the gray tide. Together they washed ashore at a point directly in front of the mural, not two feet from the blinking eyeballs in the head of the founding father.

"Oh, holy shit, this is going to be freaking great!" Billy whispered urgently. "Does she have any idea what he is trying to do to her?"

"Shut up!" Tom hissed.

Dickey wore his maniacal grin, eyes goosed open and un-blinking, never so much as shifting his gaze for a quick scan of Loretta's resplendence as they came together. He was disciplined to the point of being unnatural. His arms were outstretched and his head was cocked to one side.

"There's my girl!" he exclaimed. All looked on with beaming smiles, as if witnessing a doting father at a debutante cotillion. To Tom, Dickey looked more like a kamikaze pilot screaming toward the hull of a battleship.

Loretta threw her arms up. "Oh, Mr. Leader! You came!" She took three mincing steps toward Dickey before launching into his embrace. He leaned forward and caught her around the shoulders, hips lagging at a proper distance. The Chowderheads watched intently for every idiom in their body language, clues to the true nature of their relationship.

Dickey reached down and took her hand. He brought his free hand high above his head as they turned together to face the crowd, bringing a hush over the adoring assembly.

"Let me tell you good people that I couldn't be prouder of one of my own children than I am at this moment of our Loretta Jean!" Dickey exclaimed.

A cheer went up. Dickey again raised his hand to silence the crowd.

"Now, I know that there are those in this town who have it out for this lady," he continued, provoking a few scattered boos. Somebody hissed. "Those who are so consumed with jealousy and pettiness that they can't see that behind this pretty face there is a selfless public servant, a woman of unquestioned integrity whose sacrifice for our country is a shining example to our young people."

Loretta wore a look of breathless admiration. Dickey turned to face her. "But, Loretta, you just keep on doing the good work that you do and don't pay them no mind. Because like my ol' daddy used to say, they feed the pigeons, but they shoot the eagles! So soar high, my beautiful eagle! And let them pigeons squawk!"

The Chowderheads hollered and hooted. Dickey still held her hand, and now he raised it overhead together with his, inciting another spasm of adulation. Loretta brought the tips of her fingers to her lips in a demure gesture of humility. For a moment it wasn't hard to envision this same scene two years hence on stage at the party's presidential nominating convention.

Billy drew away from the peephole in disbelief. "*Now* tell me this guy isn't evil."

"I concede," Tom replied. That was easily the most breathtaking example of duplicity that either of them had ever seen. There was no sense trying to defend the indefensible.

"You lucky son of a bitch," Billy said.

"I don't know. This isn't quite the slam dunk that I had hoped it might be," Tom admitted. "Dickey and Stu didn't really give me enough to take straight to the air. It's a delicate dig, to say the least."

The broad outline of the story was sublime no matter which poor schlep Dickey was sacrificing. Throw in a lead character with the sex appeal of a supermarket-tabloid cover girl like Loretta Jean Polk and it was box office gold. Tom was grateful to Dickey—improbable as that seemed to him—and was enjoying a journalistic reawakening while reading up on all things Loretta.

But the dirt Dickey dished up was lacking texture. There was the allegation of insider trading and abuse of power by Loretta Jean, but none of the what, why, how, or when. What company's stock was she trading? How was she getting her information? When did she start this scam, and how much was she making off of it? Who else was in on it? Tom had fantasized over the possibilities that morning over his breakfast cereal. *Could this caper be bigger than just Loretta? My God, that would be too incredible!* Just thinking about blowing the lid off a cabal of crooked members got him juiced all over again. It would be a scandal right up there with Teapot Dome and Watergate. He'd be covered in glory. The next Bob Fucking Woodward!

It had only been twenty-four hours, but now Tom's excitement was giving way to frustration. When he pressed them to be more forthcoming with hard evidence—*at least the name of the company, for crying out loud*—both Dickey and Stu suddenly got touchy, pointing at their watches and running off to do a cable hit.

He couldn't just do the usual thing, poking around Loretta's ex-aides or fellow committee members, casually asking them if they knew anything about Loretta Jean Polk being the Bernie Madoff of the US Congress. Once word got out that he was making those kinds of calls, two things would happen. First, it would get back to Polk and any hope he had of catching her unprepared in an ambush would be gone. Second, it would take about ten minutes for the rumor mill to kick into gear once he started asking questions. Ten minutes after that happened, the story would be the talk of the press galleries. Then it was good-bye scoop. *Arrivederci* awards.

"A piece of advice?" Billy ventured. "Go down to the Legislative Reporting Center, that place where they keep all the lobbying and financial disclosure forms. Then check with the campaign finance do-gooders to see who her biggest contributors are. Find out who she's been talking to and who has been flying her where, and then do a little cross-referencing. My guess is that you'll come up with some pretty good leads in no time."

Good ol' Billy. Who in television would have thought of it but an old-time network refugee? Imagine. Actual reporting, the old fashioned way. "That, sir, is one hell of a good idea," Tom said appreciatively. "I'll be certain to thank you onstage at the awards banquet."

Dickey and Loretta were entertaining well-wishers. The horny appropriator verbally mauled them as he talked up his initiative to enclose the House chamber in bulletproof glass.

"This thing is over," Tom said to Billy. "Let's get out of here." They clambered up into the crawl space and ultimately back out into circulation amid the marbled columns of the Capitol.

Inside, the Chowderheads were dispersing. Loretta stood alone with Dickey and Stu, who spoke first. "The leader and I would like to ask you one more time to please do as we say and call it off," he said quietly to Loretta through gritted teeth. Dickey stood by, still grinning.

Loretta kept her smile wide and sweet as she put her arms around both men's necks and pulled them close.

"Fuck off," she snarled.

# Chapter 5

*In the paper today tales of war and of waste, But you*
*turn right over to the T.V. page.*

— *"Don't Dream It's Over," Crowded House*

Everyone who has ever gone to work every day has said some version of, "Truly, you can't make this shit up." Or, "I'd write a book, but no one would believe it." Tom had tinkered with a screenplay. He had the usual reporter's fantasy about hitting it big in showbiz. But the tedious absurdity of a life in the national legislature wasn't fun for anyone. After all, it was already on TV, gavel-to-gavel, and the ratings sucked.

Tom was essentially trying to sell an obsolete product to a shrinking pool of customers. His fortunes rose and fell with the number of people aged twenty-five to fifty-four years old – preferably female – who tuned in to his reporting. But the coveted demographic didn't care about the endless gridlock and infighting of Congress, so network executives didn't put reporting from Congress on their news programs. The viewer ratings were democracy in real time, capitalism in the marketplace of ideas. People voted with their remotes and their mouse clicks every minute of every day. And the apathy was endemic. When fewer than half of voters showed up to actually vote on Election Day, it was the zealots and the rich who had power and influence. When people didn't bother to vote they got what they voted for: nothing.

The zealots watched cable. Certain social media sites were the addiction of choice for the political class. And that was the nut of Tom's problem. He didn't work in cable, and he couldn't be bothered with social media. After all, he had gotten this far without it. He hated the clubhouse-clique feel of it anyway. He worked for ABN, an old-fashioned, over-the-air network. A show in the morning and another at dinnertime. It was TV news comfort food, a secluded refuge in a world changing too fast.

Politics and media were branches of the same tree. Both were risk averse, homogenized by the focus-group reign of terror. They cowered in fear of the technology revolution that had promised to democratize the media but instead only cranked up the volume on the echo chamber, leaving everyone outside the walls wondering what all the noise was about. Elections were only won and lost on the narrow fringes. Every political utterance was sliced straight from the carcass of the old way, red meat thrown to a salivating base.

As a consequence of all that, Tom was virtually anonymous. If you're a TV reporter, anonymity is bad. The world had no further use for the interpretive skills and editorial judgment of the old school. Cable news and new media were now the national steam valve, a role usurped from the long-running theatrical production known as Congress. Was it any coincidence that its members left to become cable news stars?

Tom's teenage dream was to become a famous movie director. It started with *Lion King* as a kid. By the time he was eighteen, he possessed an encyclopedic knowledge of American cinema. He planned to go to film school.

He spent freshman year hanging around the English Department, trading pretentious observations on Kubrick's use of mise-en-scène in *Paths of Glory* or Coppola's noir techniques in *The Conversation*. He couldn't watch a film without wondering why the director chose a particular framing or why he blocked out a scene the way he had.

That summer he interned in the DC ABN bureau. It wasn't film and it wasn't even fiction, but it was the closest thing to the visual arts available in DC, his hometown. And in its own way it was entertaining. He was young and impressionable, and when a veteran correspondent took a shine to him and showed him the basics, teaching him how to "hear" news as it happened and how to write a lead for a TV script, he was hooked.

He went back each summer to ABN, and by the end of junior year he figured there wasn't much more he was going to learn in college that he hadn't already absorbed through osmosis at the network. He blew off senior year and headed out to conquer America, market by market.

He paid his dues. He stood shivering outside city hall at six in the morning. He covered the water-main break, the downed power line, the contentious school board meeting and the high school championship basketball game. He was his own cameraman, soundman, and light man. He pushed the VTR button and jumped in front of the lens with a microphone, working for basically nothing and ignoring the voice in his head that told him to try and keep his johnson out of every waitress down at the local branch of the national Tex-Mex chain, where he passed as a celebrity. It was humiliating and it was hard. But Tom was young. It was bearable if you thought enough of yourself to believe you had a shot at going nationwide.

And Tom didn't lack for hubris. He had cheekbones for days, and the camera loved him. His voice carried weight. He had presence. He was full of himself, mostly owing to the fact that he hadn't yet faced serious setbacks in his career. His overconfidence was a strong point in a line of work where success can be defined by how many people hate your guts: the more the better.

He cultivated a pose of cynicism and nurtured a vague ideal—
sprung from a seed planted in his head by his hippie parents and
nurtured by a secret resentment of his old high school buddies
(salesmen of various types, all making a very enviable shitload of
money)—to forsake material gain in order do some good. So he set
out in the world seduced by the high-minded notion that journalists were an essential part of democracy, that if no one were there
to hold the feet of the powerful to the flame of accountability, then
the alluring world of pork, politics, and power would lead to corruption. He would stand in the breach and defend democracy from
crooked kleptocracy.

He accepted as an article of faith that a free and obnoxious
press was a major reason why the Republic had stood for two-
hundred-some-odd years. He happily bounced around in the
faces of mayors, councilmen, commissioners, and big shots, asking meddlesome questions and daring them to lose their tempers
on camera. It gained him notoriety and attention from network
scouts and TV news talent agents, and so he cast himself as a
righteous defender of the public interest. A real reporter.

But in Washington things weren't working out for him on
any level. So much of what he did as a journalist was simply re-
packaging and aggregating what had happened in public hours
before the ABN newscast. By the time he got on the air at the
end of the day the story he reported had already ricocheted
around the Internet for most of the day. At that point, anyone who really cared about politics had moved on to the next

bright shiny object. Everyone else, the vast majority, simply weren't interested.

By now Tom's sense of purpose was eroded, its sediment now a silty layer of sarcasm and resentment for the whole business of Washington. Whatever was left of his sense of mission was buried underneath.

# CHAPTER 6

Two months before Dickey had made his deal with Tom, Cornelia Livingwell sat in a rooftop bistro in Adams Morgan and sobbed.

"My life has become a nightmare," Cornelia whimpered. "My father has lost his way. He's a monster."

Loretta Jean Polk was her companion that day. Half a glass into the bottle of Sancerre on the table between them and Cornelia was choking on bitter regret.

"He's worse than selfish!" she wailed. "He treats me like a commodity to be traded, a token in his stupid power game. I have no control over who I am!"

Cornelia was talking about her father, Zach Dickey.

"You have to stand up to him. You have to say no, for both your sakes," Loretta counseled.

"How can I? I'm totally dependent on him. He controls everything in my life!" Cornelia was disconsolate. Her childhood had been a journey along campaign trails laid end to end. Waving from the back of convertibles, speaking to ladies' clubs back home, canvassing, and passing out campaign fliers door to door. Standing sentry, a terra-cotta princess at her father's shoulder as delivered his stem-winders. There was Cornelia, almost motionless, cueing the clueless in the crowd with nods or animatronic laughter at stories a thousand times told, a sturdy totem of piety.

It all just came naturally. She shared in the joy of her father's triumphs. And her status as his daughter opened doors. Front-row concert seats and airplane upgrades. Countless perks, big and small. Jobs. Salary. Respect. She had loved every minute, as she had loved her father. But it was different now.

She saw what this life did to her mother. The subservience, the phoniness, the faux fulfillment when in truth a lifetime of being taken for granted—sacrificed on the altar of her husband's ambition—had left her depressed and living on a diet of Rusty Nails and Zoloft. Over the years, Cornelia had grown to hate her. Now she only felt pity.

Cornelia saw herself heading down that same path. But now it was no longer simply about the desire for a more normal life outside politics. She was done being an accessory in his political wardrobe. The role of accomplice to the usual Machiavellian intrigue had grown to be unbearable. She had a desperate need to

escape the reflected pallor of her father's limelight. Th
of a presidential campaign was enough to send her to
week.

But now she was being asked—no, *told*—to be party t
thing more nefarious. Something that was clearly criminal
her father asked of her brought on bouts of nausea.

# CHAPTER 7

*The most important thing is honesty. Once you can fake*
*that, you've got it made.*

—*George Burns*

**Zach Dickey understood** one of the essential ironies of politics: the
people who most fear your power are the same people with the
power to take it away. The trick is to make them think they have
a stake in keeping you at the top, to play on their sense of loyalty
until they think they somehow owe you something, instead of
vice versa.

Dickey had a powerful enemy. The CEO of Minton Systems
was working behind the scenes to back a Dickey rival in early
maneuvering for the Iowa caucuses. When he discovered this
treachery, Dickey was apoplectic and threatened retribution. He
would block earmarks, starve the company of pork, and revoke

its tax breaks and its generous helpings of corporate welfare. He would pressure regulators and see to it that Minton would owe millions more in taxes. He would go out of his way to tie the company up in regulatory red tape. He swore to expose the CEO as a political meddler, an untenable position for a man leading a publicly held company with stockholders—and customers—of every political stripe.

The Minton man initially backed away, swearing off allegiance to the Dickey rival and, in a gesture of contrition, agreed to take on Dickey's daughter, Cornelia, in his Washington lobby shop. She would serve as both hostage and spy in a rival fiefdom. It was an arrangement worthy of the Borgias.

But the CEO loved the game too much. He imagined himself kingmaker and puppeteer, a potential plutocrat. If Dickey actually had a shot at going all the way, then fine. He'd be with Dickey. But he judged otherwise. He came to realize he didn't have to worry about any damage to Minton's brand. The wealthy were expected to pull the strings. At this moment in popular culture the cloak of neutrality was moth-eaten, threadbare. He could take a public stand and spend what he liked. America had entered a new Gilded Age.

Government contracts, a favorable tax and regulatory environment…if he succeeded in the role of Oval Office power broker, the possibilities for him and his company were limitless. All it took was a little luck and money, and that amounted to pocket change. The ante for influence in Washington was less than what he paid one Minton plant worker in a year. The risk/reward ratio was off the charts. It was a no-brainer.

Though he was no longer concerned with what the public thought, the Minton CEO knew that the majority leader of the US House was still a man to be reckoned with. So he tried to sneak his betrayal through surrogates and use dark-money donations in the foolish hope that he could keep that kind of activity a secret from a man as connected as Dickey.

Inevitably and quickly, he was discovered. The feud was back on. This time Dickey would not be satisfied with anything less than the utter destruction of the Minton CEO. And if that meant bringing down Minton itself—a too-big-to-fail titan of American commerce of four generations—well, if that was the way it had to be, then so be it. Dickey hardly gave it a thought.

So he put the arm on his daughter, Cornelia, to use her position within Minton and come up with inside dirt that might be of interest to the SEC, the FTC, the IRS…whatever. Bookkeeping rigmarole, shady options deals, or something especially outrageous on the CEO's compensation package. Or his personal life. Kinks, twists…anything, the more explosive the better. In the meantime, he encouraged the most trusted members of his political syndicate in Washington and Tennessee—all of whom happened to be frequent donors to his various campaigns and related endeavors—to short Minton stock in anticipation of a scandal that would drive the price through the floor. They stood to make a windfall, and Dickey figured on a percentage.

But Cornelia refused to cooperate. She'd had enough.

Her father wouldn't take no for an answer. She went to Stu Albertson and begged him to convince her father to leave her out of it. Stu agonized, torn between his allegiance to Dickey and his benign affection for Cornelia. In the end he decided not to decide.

So Cornelia turned to Loretta Jean Polk and here she was, gulping down mouthfuls of wine and spilling her guts in Adams Morgan. Despite all the noise around her, her beauty and her celebrity and her life of tabloid fodder, Loretta had always been a kind heart and willing listener. There had been times when Cornelia had suspected her ambition, and others her sincerity. But her father had recognized Loretta's potential as an ally long ago and had nurtured her career from the start. She was a member in good standing in the Dickey syndicate. Cornelia hoped that maybe she could talk to him and make him stop.

"This is bullshit!" Loretta exclaimed, indignant. Her outrage wasn't just empathy for a troubled acquaintance. Dickey was trying to drag her into the same swamp. Two days earlier he had asked Loretta to use her position as subcommittee chairman to call a hearing on trumped-up charges of bookkeeping shenanigans at Minton. She didn't know why until now.

For Loretta, it went beyond disgust with Dickey's garden-variety scheming and corruption. A man exploiting a woman close to him? His own daughter? Taking her for granted? Wrapping her in disused bonds of love, no matter how corroded by years of neglect, to drag her along a ruinous path into a criminal conspiracy? And all for the sake of more power. It was never enough.

Loretta took it personally. She'd been dodging these traps every step of the way, from the plains of Wyoming to the Capitol Dome. From her own father to her deceased husband, the men in her life offered no empowerment, only the burden of expectation: to perform, to support, to clean up after the mess left by their thoughtless megalomania. Projecting a stoic masculinity that they took as license to ignore her. As a young woman she had blamed herself. She was conditioned to believe that she was defective, incapable of succeeding without the benevolent shelter of a big, strong presence to guide her, to keep her infantilized and ignorant. Those weren't relationships. They were a one-way street heading toward a life wasted in frustration. She only existed to service their narcissism.

And so here was another arrogant alpha male feeding on the very love he needed to flourish, a virus exploiting its host. Fathers don't ruin their daughters' lives for the sake of ambition. Her response to Cornelia's story was to project the ancient resentments she had for her father and her late husband onto Zach Dickey.

Loretta had long since learned to cope with her hatred for her father and husband and had moved on. She had achieved enlightenment, while dear Cornelia sat before her brooding in the dark. Loretta resolved to fix that. They would take a stand together, shoulder to shoulder, and fight.

They polished off the Sancerre then switched up grapes and regions, ordering a Puligny Montrachet and appetizers to share. They talked for hours, and when it was time to go, they stood on wobbly legs and embraced.

A few tables away a plainclothes Capitol policeman held his phone to his ear, trying to stay perfectly still and fix his gaze on a point roughly ninety degrees from where the two women sat. He wasn't making a call. He was framing them up in his camera lens, and as the pair lingered in each other's arms, he sent the live stream of the scene back to Leader Dickey, alone at his desk in the Capitol.

# CHAPTER 8

*Things ain't what they used to be,*
*and probably never was.*

—*Will Rogers*

Washington was the pinnacle of TV news, and Capitol Hill was one foothold below the summit, the White House. A few years back, when Tom first arrived on the beat, he couldn't sleep knowing the next day he was to interview Senator or Congressman So-and-So. He stayed up late rehearsing his questions, practicing his introductions. It was important to be aggressive, edgy. He hated himself when he fawned over the powerful as if he were again eighteen and politicians were the guys in the E Street Band.

He wasn't naïve. It was just a touch of Potomac fever that cleared his jaundiced eye. He took to watching Saturday-night reruns of think-tank symposia and regarded himself an expert on the latest insurance reform initiative or the energy and water appropriations bill. The irony of Washington was that though it self-consciously clung to its role as latter-day Athens—stands of Corinthian pillars of no structural value evoking classical ideals of democratic rule by the masses—the town cultivated an air of diffidence and superiority. Tom was seduced by the whole atmosphere of the place. For the first time in his life he felt inadequate.

He tried to compensate. He engaged in the esoterica of policy, hoping to be accepted in the salons of political power—thought at the time to be located somewhere in Georgetown north of N Street and east of Wisconsin Avenue—and ultimately judged worthy of initiation into the secret cabal that ran things. He just assumed that these people were Serious Thinkers—it all just came off too smoothly for there not to be some kind of learned deliberation somewhere along the line—and so he reinvented himself as a think-tank brainiac.

New York network bosses had experience with this syndrome, and it mystified them. They always wondered why smart people would swoon over a quaint little company town like Washington.

It took about three months of Tom pitching stories so dense with Washingtonspeak that they would have been rejected by Congressional Quarterly before a producer mocked Tom on a conference call, sarcastically asking for an update on the Small Business Committee markup, and wondering if Tom could go live for a network break-in during its most popular afternoon soap opera for a report on the final vote.

Now Tom's nest egg was oozing away into a stream of corporate malfeasance. His career track had become a garbage-strewn gulley. He tried to think of ways to rekindle some of the old crusader's ardor. He could try his hand at financial reporting. That was fertile ground for the righteous. But he was paralyzed by the abiding disdain he had for the politicians he had come to hold in such low regard.

He had come too far to be made a laughing stock. He wasn't going back to Fargo—or some damned place—to spend the rest of his life as a big-haired local anchor clad in sport-coat ensembles ripped from the yellowed pages of the Johnny Carson Collection catalogue. He resolved to do whatever was needed, including making deals with the likes of Zach Dickey. If that's what it took to stay in Washington, he would do it.

# CHAPTER 9

"This is room B-109," the clerk whispered into the receiver. "The books are ready for pickup."

It was the coded signal he had agreed on at his first and only meeting with the woman on the other end of the line, and now the eager apparatchik's heart raced as he eyed Tom Salta from behind the reception desk.

"How long?"

"Came in just five minutes ago," replied the clerk. "I thought it was best to wait awhile before I picked up the phone and called, just to be safe." This was only the second time he had personally spoken to Congresswoman Polk, and he was a nervous wreck. "I didn't want to be too obvious and tip him off," he added conspiratorially. He was trying to remember if Loretta had assigned him a code name.

"Very good thinking, Irv. Did he sign in? What is the name on your sheet?"

Irv glanced down at the signature on the document request list. "Hugh G. Rection," he reported. Then, "Oh."

"That's OK. They're all smart-asses. It's to be expected. You're doing a great job. Just tell me what he looks like and we'll take it from there." On some level Irv knew that he was being patronized, but he was powerless to raise an objection in the face of a personal entreaty from Loretta Jean Polk.

She had come to him out of the blue a few days back with a proposition: if anyone, especially a journalist, came in asking for her financial and travel disclosure forms, he was to call her directly on her personal cell phone.

As a rule, Irv went out of his way to avoid contact with members of Congress. It wasn't that he held them in low regard. Quite the opposite. He was very much in awe of them, intimidated by their power and authority. Familiarity with members could only threaten his comfortable anonymity. Irv was of the old school that still held that the stability of a government job—with its security, pension, and benefits—was the best way to go in life. The backslapping world of the cloakroom was an unknown variable that Irv, not a naturally curious man nor consumed with ambition, saw no reason to be a part of.

His one and only interaction with an elected representative had come when he had a brief job interview with the chairman whose committee controlled the operations of the Legislative Reporting Center and the rest of the Capitol infrastructure. The chairman's position was historically coveted by committee members for its opportunities to extend influence through patronage jobs, much like the one that brought Irv here to the Hill. In Irv's case, the chairman had needed a favor involving a project in his largely agricultural district (federal dollars appropriated for a fifty-foot statue in front of city hall depicting the Roman goddess Robigo, protector of the corn crop) from another committee chairman, and since Irv's mother was the first cousin of the second chairman's third wife, a connection was made.

He got the job. It was a minor transaction in the vast network of chits and favors that were the underpinning of the political infrastructure. That was nineteen years ago, and he had been toiling there in blissful obscurity ever since. It was also the last time he had spoken directly to a member, until Loretta came floating in the other day to personally deliver her updated disclosure forms.

Irv was overwhelmed by the presence of such a renowned beauty who also happened to be a congresswoman. Her eyes fell on him the moment she walked in, holding him in her gaze and rendering him immobile as she approached with an extended hand. From there his recollection of the encounter got hazy, like a fighter knocked senseless in the first round only to come to later in the dressing room and be told that he had gone the distance. At that moment he understood that the memory of this one meeting would stay with him for years, engendering an epoch of self-abuse that would be yet one more thing in his life that was beyond his control.

"About six foot. Dark hair. Big chin. Looks kind of like a member himself," Irv told her.

"Would you consider him to be handsome? What color are his eyes?"

Irv's heart sank. *She thinks I'm gay. His eyes?*

"Think for a second, Irv. He must have flashed a credential. Is he print or broadcast?"

*Of course. The credential.* "Um. It was ABN. I remember because the first thing I thought of when I saw it was how they have the best weatherman on that channel. The fat one with the blond hair."

"Thank you. You've been wonderful. I'm not going to forget this." She hung up.

If sunshine really was the best disinfectant, then it stood to reason that the Legislative Reporting Center was located in a windowless Capitol Hill basement. In an age when every member of Congress and their staff had every e-mail, Tweet, Facebook post, and sundry message announce its arrival on the cell phones they wore on their belts like some sort of vibrating codpiece, the Legislative Reporting Center was the last redoubt in the monastic tradition of handwritten documentation. Another opaque layer of bureaucracy thrown over the public's right to transparency in the government that they paid for.

If you really wanted to know who was lobbying whom and what companies were providing planes to golf tournaments; what front group for the Taiwanese government was picking up the bill to send hordes of staffers to the Far East to expose them to the virtues of the island nation; how much a member made in stock dividends from the Fortune 500 company founded by her great-grandfather that happened to be affected by every other piece of legislation that hit the floor; or whose spouse was a lobbyist himself, then you had to find your way through Capitol security and down to this nondescript cavern to leaf through thousands of pages of hard copy to find it.

A sign some wag had hung in the TV reporters' gallery years before read, "Get out there and scratch the surface!" It was a dose of self-deprecating sarcasm. Every other branch of journalism regarded TV folk as superficial lightweights. Like oppressed peoples through the millennia, TV journos had co-opted the worst stereotype and turned it into a battle cry. The sign had become a talisman, touched by reporters for good luck as they filed past, a ritual pregnant with the kind of bitter irony that sustained them.

Now Tom sat in a Legislative Reporting Center carrel, buried in reams of documents and waiting for the clue that would unlock the mystery of Loretta's corruption to jump out and bite him in the ass. He was a TV guy, after all. This kind of painstaking forensic journalism was not his strong suit. Was reporting really all about digging through obscure and monotonous files? Human source intelligence—that was his milieu. Mingling with the elites and pretending to be a policy maven he could do, but sitting around up to his elbows in disclosure forms trying to find a needle in a haystack was downright depressing. He had been there for maybe ten minutes.

Tom thought of a story his Uncle Dominic used to tell of the time he was thirteen years old and growing up in Takoma Park. Uncle Dom found himself penniless in a record store the day his hero, Bruce Springsteen, released *Darkness on the Edge of Town*. Bruce was on the album cover in a black leather jacket and a greaser's white T-shirt, staring back at Tom's uncle with the coal-black eyes of a fugitive. A clerk behind the counter cranked up the volume on "Badlands," and when the Boss declared that he didn't give a damn for just the in-betweens, Uncle Dom knew what he had to do. He picked up three copies and ran out the door.

As a young man hearing his uncle tell the story, Tom had envisioned the scene in vivid detail. Now it flashed in Tom's mind once more as he glanced over his shoulder at Irv. Running through the halls of Congress with Loretta's files was totally impractical. They weighed at least thirty pounds. On the other hand, this business about spending weeks sleuthing and slogging was pretty much a nonstarter. No matter the potential payoff down the line, he just didn't have that kind of discipline.

He unholstered his cell phone and dialed Billy's number.

"BOP. O'Nesti." Sometimes working with Billy made Tom feel like a bit player in *His Girl Friday*.

"I'd like to order up a little diversion."

"I live to serve," said Billy, ever quick on the uptake. "What shall it be this time? I'm running a special on thunderous flatulence this week. Guaranteed to change the dynamic in any room."

"I'll leave the particulars to your discretion. Why don't you come on down to the LRC and show a little leg to the nerd behind the desk? I'm going to be making an unauthorized withdrawal."

Eight minutes later Billy was standing before Irv. "So let me get this straight. You are refusing to provide me with *both* the earthquake machine budget *and* the mistress disclosure forms? Is that an accurate characterization of your position? Because I'm going to break this story wide open if it is!"

"Sir, I'm not sure what you—"

"So you're denying the existence of the machine? What is the correct spelling of your name?"

*It's all coming crashing down,* thought Irv. *This is what I get for thinking I had it made.* "I don't think you understand the mission of our—"

"Oh, I'm all too aware of your mission," Billy said. He was up on his toes and had one eyebrow arched. "And as long as you brought it up, I want to speak to the director. Get him down here!"

"The director?" Now Irv was really confused. He was about to go get his boss to handle this situation anyway. But his title was administrator, not director.

"Do I have to spell it out for you? The director. The DCI. Of the CIA. The guy who is pulling the strings on this whole operation!"

"Ah. The director. Yes. One moment please." *A conspiracy nut.* Irv had finally caught on. "I'll just go in the back and bring him right out."

Tom quickly tucked away two random binders and headed for the door. "Bravo, my good man!" he whispered to Billy.

"No charge, my friend." He fell in behind Tom, and together they disappeared into the Capitol's catacombs.

# Chapter 10

"**O**ld School! My man!" Tom greeted the hunched figure of Gil Jorgensen as he breezed into the TV reporters' gallery bright and early on Monday morning. He was in an expansive mood.

"So, Gil, what are you hearing? Did they pass that resolution supporting the goals and ideals of Mr. Rogers last night after I left?"

Gil had been a swaggering network cowboy who rode the bucking bronco for eight years as Washington bureau chief for the storied CNB News before the constant network infighting finally caught up to him. In the end—for lack of anything else to do with him—they exiled him to the journalistic Elba known as the US House of Reprehensibles.

Gil was always the first one in the gallery, grunting a greeting to each later arrival as he grimly hunched at his computer reading in on overnight news. Tom wasn't above having a laugh at Gil's expense and considered his style and approach to television news to be hilariously outdated. Yet there was something about the man that Tom loved. Gil showed up at the Capitol each morning in freshly shined shoes and cufflinks, a sharp Brylcreem-reinforced part in his hair. Every night he stayed at his post until the House went out of session, no matter how trivial the legislation being debated. He maintained an endearing refusal to carry a cell phone. The guy was Perry Como in a Pit Bull world, a walking anachronism. Tom both admired and felt sorry for him.

"One 'nay' vote. Towney said he couldn't support it. Said Mr. Rogers advocated a homosexual lifestyle," Gil reported. He still hadn't looked up from his computer.

"That would explain a lot. I grew up watching Mr. Rogers," Tom allowed. "No wonder I'm not married. It turns out I spent my childhood being bombarded by subliminal suggestions of deviance."

"Well, now you know," Gil said to his screen.

Rejection was still an unusual experience for Tom. He didn't know when to quit.

"Personally, I always had my suspicions about Mr. Greenjeans."

"Yeah," Gil muttered.

Tom wasn't giving up. "Hey, you won't believe what they sent me from the bureau yesterday." He reached into his go-bag and rummaged. "They told us that we have to have this with us at all times, as long as we're in the Capitol."

Tom pulled a black rubber gas mask out of the bag and held it up for Gil's inspection. It was an elaborate apparatus, a hood with straps hanging from it like a tangle of clematis, and a large silver canister for a nose. Each network had requisitioned the masks after 9/11 and the anthrax attacks on the Capitol. Tom and his colleagues would periodically receive an updated model, sent from their bosses back in the DC bureaus. "Shit, between this thing and the chemical hoods they passed out last month, you'd almost think it wasn't safe to work here," he said.

Gil still hadn't looked up, so Tom put the mask on over his head, pulled the straps tight, and launched into a muffled rendition of "Old Folks at Home," Al Jolson style.

Tom saw Gil's lips move. He was apparently trying to say something, but Tom couldn't hear a thing. He took the mask off and leaned in close. "What's that? You say you have a request for 'Toot Toot Tootsie'?"

"I said I think you have a visitor." Gil raised a finger in the direction of Tom's booth.

Tom turned to see a poorly shod foot bobbing on the end of a man's crossed leg poking out from his doorway. A bunched and sodden argyle sagged around the ankle. As he entered his booth Tom knew who was waiting without having to see the rest of what was certain to be a sartorial disaster.

"So. A rare foray into enemy territory," Tom greeted Stu. He closed the door behind him. "Are you sure you want to be seen up here in my booth? I mean, when this thing breaks, people are going to put two and two together. It's no skin off my chin if people know where I got the story, but I was under the impression that I was supposed to be Secret Squirrel to your Boris Badanov."

Stu's lips were pinched and bloodless. He was even more pallid than usual.

Tom shifted uneasily. "Jesus Christ, man, we have got to get you out into the sunshine. An injection of vitamin D and shit. You look ghastly." He worried about the lack of ventilation in the cramped space. The way Stu looked, he didn't even want to be breathing the same air.

Stu raised a news clipping covered in yellow highlights and held it six inches from Tom's face. "We are starting to be very disappointed in you, Tom."

"Congresswoman: SUVs Endanger Seniors," read the screamer. It was an article printed from BOP's website, essentially a transcript of a story that had been running on their air all morning. A link to the video was provided in the margin.

A photograph of Representative Polk featured prominently near the top of the page.

Tom made an effort to look unimpressed. "Nice little hit for BOP," he offered. "But what does this have to do with us?"

Stu exhaled heavily. "When we gave you the other story—and need I remind you that we are now talking about almost a full week gone by—we thought at this point the only front-page picture of her would be from her perp walk down at the federal lockup," he said tersely. "Instead, we wake up this morning to find that here she is, the righteous defender of little old ladies. So my question to you is, what's the holdup? What is keeping you from getting off your ass and slam-dunking this bitch on national television like we asked you to do?"

Tom had to wonder again just what in the hell had she done to them. "Why don't you calm down?" he suggested. "It's just some penny-ante news-you-can-use bullshit."

That was the front. Inwardly Tom was wondering how he had missed out. His superiors loved this kind of chestnut, just the sort of trifle perfect for the A block of the evening news. Tom would hear an earful on the morning's conference call about not having it first, no doubt. There would be the requisite lecture about the importance of behind the scenes access to members of Congress, and how ABN needed to be first in line at the spigot of leaked reports.

He would have to call Billy and get to the bottom of this thing. There had to be an explanation for the story showing up on BOP with no heads-up from his partner in crime. The piece was based on a Government Accountability Office report—commissioned by none other than Loretta Jean—that found a disproportionate number of SUV-related traffic accidents involved senior citizens. The precise cause of this phenomenon was unclear, but the report's authors speculated that seniors tended to panic when their view of the roadway was blocked by the oversized vehicles and overreact by taking evasive measures: dangerously swerving into other lanes, or worse, oncoming traffic. BOP, i.e., Billy, had evidently gotten an advance copy leaked to them two days in advance of public release.

Like Tom had said—a nice little hit. It didn't take a genius to figure out what sold a spot to the evening news. Anything that had to do with seniors was a lock to get on the air. They were the only folks who were actually home in front of the TV at 6:30 p.m., or who hadn't seen the same story hours before on the Internet. Loretta Jean had ordered up the Government Accountability Office study with the full hope and expectation that it would get her a couple of days of play on the evening news. She was savvy like that.

"Let me make this as clear as I can for you," Stu continued, making an obvious effort to contain his anger. "The leader does not want this to drag on any longer than necessary. Therefore, I have been authorized to tell you the following: from here on out we want a daily progress report on where you are in this story and what you have done to break it. That includes a list of calls you have made, documents you have obtained, and people you have met with."

"Get fucking serious," Tom scoffed. Mutual exploitation was one thing. But he wasn't so desperate that he would allow himself to become another one of Dickey's pathetic stooges like his visitor here.

"Oh, I can assure you that we're serious. And if you feel somehow that these conditions violate your very high-minded sense of journalistic ethics, then we will understand completely and see if your good friend Billy O'Nesti can do something with this story."

Tom felt the rage gland release the day's first fix into his bloodstream. "I have a better idea. Instead of showing up here and trying to order me around like I'm one of Dickey's mafia foot soldiers, why don't *you* supply *me* with a list of people I should call, documents that I need, and people to meet with? Because as long as we're talking, Stu, I have to tell you that you guys haven't given me jack shit to go on."

Stu rolled his eyes. "What kind of world do you live in that someone just hands you the opportunity of a lifetime, and instead of working around the clock to cash in, you take the weekend off? You come waltzing in here on Monday morning, and you and I both know that you haven't lifted a finger on this story for two days."

That was a clean-hit punch to the midsection. Tom was briefly deflated. He really had meant to work on it over the weekend, but of course he had forgotten to bring his stolen folder home on Friday and didn't realize it until Saturday afternoon, by which time he was out in Annapolis having a big time with his old high school buddies, up to his elbows in crab goo, a pitcher of Sam Adams sloshing around in his belly.

He thought it best to dispute the premise. "You have no idea what journalism is. You think that I can just go on the air and repeat an allegation without attribution and no evidence whatsoever?"

"Sure I do. We told you what the story was. That's all the confirmation you need. It happens all the time."

"And it's journalistic McCarthyism, not even fit for a supermarket tabloid," said Tom, falling back to the moral high ground, familiar territory when he was losing an argument. "I know that's what passes for news on cable. But I can't go around just repeating rumors posted on some shady website," he said. "We're not talking about scoring some cheap points by calling her a liberal. We're talking about a federal crime and a serious breach of the public trust. If I did as you suggest then the only person whose career would be in ruins would be my own, assuming that they would even let me on the air to begin with."

This didn't seem to register with Stu. He tossed the clippings aside and leaned back in Tom's chair. "Level with me. Has she gotten to you? We all know that she is a very seductive woman. Are you giving her a break for some reason?"

Tom chuckled. For a moment Stu had had him going, that he was serious about giving the story away to someone else. Now it was obvious that the man was simply not thinking rationally.

"I could not give a shit if Loretta Jean Polk drops dead tomorrow," Tom declared with proud indignation. "Wait. Let me amend that. I could not give a shit if she drops dead in jail, after my story airs."

"That's fine, Tom. But that really isn't an answer to my question."

"What are you asking me then? Am I fucking her? Because if that's what you're asking then I want to hear those words come out of your mouth."

"*You* screwing *her* is not as likely as vice versa, but OK. Are you having sex with Loretta Polk?"

This was a side of Stu that Tom would have never thought existed. "No. You can leave my booth now."

"Come on, Tom. If you knew her like I know her, the question wouldn't seem out of line."

The rage-a-hol was now at flood stage. "Are you paranoid or just delusional?" he fumed. "You guys think that every wild accusation that you make can be justified because everyone is so obviously out to get you. If she isn't swinging by a rope three minutes after you order her execution, it's because either I've been compromised or the liberal media cabal has ordained that she be spared. Well, I'm calling bullshit on that!"

Stu slid meekly down into his seat in the face of the barrage. Tom sensed that this was the time to press his advantage.

"Don't you understand that I need hard, bona fide proof of her corruption?" He lowered his voice in an attempt to appear reasonable. "Now, instead of sitting there in my ergonomic chair and making lewd accusations, how about giving me the supporting detail that I need for this story?"

"OK, OK," Stu said. "Let me have a look at those documents that you stole from the LRC the other day."

That brought Tom up short, but he couldn't help but laugh. "I'm sure I don't know what you're talking about." *Sometimes you really do have to admire these guys*, he thought. "But humor me. What makes you think I have any such documents?"

"Please, Tom. Don't even ask, because you don't want to know."

Fair enough and probably true. Tom reached up to a shelf above Stu's head and grabbed the binder. "For the record, your characterization of how I came into possession of these documents is inaccurate," he said as he sheepishly handed them over. "I do have scruples."

"Tell it to the sergeant at arms," Stu laughed. "But I might mention that your scruples look pretty dubious on the security footage. Especially during the part where you're stuffing a binder under your jacket. You did everything but say 'cheese.'"

Tom hadn't bothered to think about the ubiquitous surveillance cameras when he and Billy were running out the door as giddy as eighth graders. Some master criminal.

"Let's never speak of it again," Tom said.

Stu was already going through the documents. He paused briefly over a few of the pages, but began flipping through again before Tom could determine what, precisely, had attracted his interest. Tom was practiced in the art of reading upside down. It was an essential skill, brought into play when he found himself standing before an important member's desk. But Stu was already handing the binder back.

"Well, I hope you got some jollies from lifting this stuff," Stu said. "Because the smoking gun isn't there."

"That brings us to square one, now doesn't it?" Tom said. "I don't understand why you're making me jump through all these hoops when you obviously have the power to just give me what I need now. I could be on the air tonight."

Stu still wasn't looking him in the eye. "It's not that simple," he mumbled.

"Why not? I mean, I know I work in television and all, but that doesn't mean that I'm so stupid that I can't see she has somehow fucked you guys so badly that you're determined to ruin her. Gimme a little credit."

Stu tugged at his argyles. "I'm not going to say that you're right or wrong. I'm not going to talk about it either way." He stood to leave.

Tom took a side step to block his path. They were chest to chest. "But don't you see? That's exactly the point!" Tom whispered urgently. "We don't *have* to talk about it, because I don't give a *damn* what she did to you. It makes no difference to me whatsoever! Just give me the goods and she goes down."

Stu looked like he was thinking it over.

"Sit back down," Tom instructed. He sensed he could close the deal. Stu sat.

"We wouldn't have to meet face to face," Tom pressed. He could see the wheels turning in Stu's head. "Just give me what you think I need. We'll work out a dead drop somewhere."

Stu still hedged. "I don't know. Let me talk it over with the leader."

"Why does he need to know? He obviously trusts you to do whatever it takes to get the job done. That's all he cares about: the bottom line. Think about it, man. This way he has plausible deniability. No fingerprints. You would be doing him a favor by not consulting him."

Stu began to waver. Here he was in the ABN booth, of all places, allowing himself to be talked further into a conspiracy with the likes of a spineless worm like Tom Salta. He had been against this ludicrous scheme to begin with, but Dickey insisted that if they kept their cool and played the hand through then things would work out. Now they were blowing through one warning sign after another, and Stu feared they were heading straight for a cliff.

"Let's take a dry run," Tom suggested.

"Huh?"

"A dry run. You leave me some dummy docs at the drop—"

"Hold on a minute. What drop? I haven't agreed to—"

"Good point. How about the Ohio Clock? Just leave the docs in the belly of the thing, where senators hid their hooch during prohibition."

"Oh, for chrissakes."

"Just a first installment. So you can get comfortable."

"That's not a dry run."

"OK. Let's call it a down payment." Stu was born to be a straight man. Something about him always made Tom feel puckish.

"That doesn't make me feel any better."

"OK. What would you like to call it?"

"Call what? We haven't agreed to anything yet."

"Exactly. That's why it's a dry run."

Stu's head was spinning. "OK, look. I'll play your game, but I don't see any point in this foolishness with a dry run or the Ohio Clock. Why can't we just meet here tomorrow morning?"

"You don't want that and I don't want that. It's already bad enough that you're here." Tom tilted his head toward the booth door. "I'm sure rumors are flying around in the gallery now, as we speak."

"But the Ohio Clock? It's so dime-store thriller. Not to mention obvious."

"It really is rather cinematic. I think that's why I like it," Tom replied.

Stu remained silent.

"Fine," Tom sighed. "So send a page. What will be the signal?"

"The signal?"

"Yeah, the signal. To let me know when to look." At this point Tom was practically channeling Lou Costello.

"Great. Now I'm Whittaker Chambers."

"He had nicer clothes."

Stu exhaled wearily. "We don't need a signal," he said finally. "Forget this nonsense about a dry run. The whole package will be there by the time the bells go off for the first vote tomorrow."

"Perfect." Tom grinned a self-satisfied grin.

"You're still going to need help reading it."

"Oh, jeez." More dry research. "Can't you just mark the juicy parts with Post-its?"

"I was just about to ask you the same thing." Stu got up and took a step toward the door, then abruptly stopped. Reaching across Tom's face, he punched up the volume on the TV.

The BOP story was running yet again, and here was Loretta about to deliver her sound bite. The harsh TV lights were masked with warm gels. Her eyes glistened with the benefit of a small halogen set up next to the lens. Her luxuriant hair was set off to perfection by a backlight, and the focus was just soft enough to set her aglow and still be suitable for a news story. Stu recognized the star treatment and became incensed all over again.

"More and more of these enormous vehicles are on the roads, and something must be done to ensure the safety and well-being of our seniors," Loretta said earnestly, her voice brimming with empathy. "Therefore, I have submitted legislation that will establish a pilot program, directing states to train those over sixty-five on how to drive SUVs."

Tom prepared to duck in case Stu threw something. Instead, he became eerily calm.

"Tomorrow at first bells," he said and walked out the door. Five of Tom's competitors poked their heads out of their booths to watch him go.

Tom fell back into his chair, pleased with his manipulations. Then he felt the damp warmth of Stu's lingering presence seeping through his blazer and leapt up in revulsion.

# Chapter 11

If you aren't careful, healthy skepticism will harden into malignant disgust. Dismiss everything as spin and then, sooner or later, you miss something real. Maybe something big. Something that can make a career.

The booth phone rang with the morning's conference call, and Tom, as was his habit, put it on speaker and hit the mute button. He braced himself for a scolding.

"Good morning, everyone!" It was the senior show producer for the evening news. "Tom Salta, are you on the call?

They were coming to him first. Which meant they were really pissed. Tom turned off mute. "Salta is on," he said, trying to sound sanguine.

"Good news, bad news, Tom," the New York producer began. "There is an excellent story out there today on seniors and SUVs, and we'd like for you to take a whack at it for to-night's show."

"Can do!" Tom chirped. The other booth line began to ring. He lifted the receiver and in the same motion slammed it back into its cradle.

"The bad news is that a pissant little cable outfit had it before we did." The producer's tone grew menacing. "I'm not going to get into it too far with you now, Tom. But suffice to say that ABN does not get beaten by some half-ass double-A farm team. As an ABN correspondent you need to have better access to those people down there. The next story to be broken on the Hill will be broken on this network and on this show. Are we clear?"

"Understood." This was a time to play good soldier. Salute and keep marching.

"OK then. Let's go on to Chicago. What's news in the Windy City?"

*Fucking New York. Fucking Dickey. Fucking Loretta. Fuck them all.* Hatred boiled up into Tom's neck.

The booth extension rang again and Tom snapped it up.

"What?"

"Um, is this Tom Salta?"

"Yeah. Who are you?"

"Please hold for Congresswoman Polk."

Tom hung up.

It rang again. Tom stared at the blinking light for a moment before he picked up the receiver and silently put it to his ear.

"Tom?" It was her.

He didn't answer.

"Tom, this is Loretta Jean Polk. I think it's time that we met."

He wasn't ready for this. "Well, if this is about the SUV story, then you're a day late."

"YOU'RE GODDAMN RIGHT IT'S A DAY LATE!" screamed the New York producer through the speakerphone that Tom had forgotten to put back on mute.

"Some people are trying to give you bad information," Loretta continued.

"It wouldn't be the first time."

"I'd like to appeal to your sense of journalistic fairness. We need to meet. You owe me that."

Tom hesitated. There really wasn't much upside to meeting her now. Too premature. She was just trying to soften him up. "I owe you? For what? Screwing me on the SUV story?"

"Please?"

Tom wanted to resist, or at least put her off. "Tomorrow," he said.

"It can't wait until tomorrow. Meet me now. There are things that you need to know."

He began to rationalize. Maybe she had something on Dickey that she wanted to trade. He had sworn that he didn't care what was between them. But still. Who knew where it all could lead? It would be prudent to keep the doors of opportunity open. They would meet, and if she had something good, he could take it from there. If not, if she were simply trying to soften him up, then there was nothing keeping him from walking away. His resolve began to melt. What harm could it do?

"OK, you win. I'll be in your office in ten minutes."

"Not my office, they're watching this place. Meet me on the mezzanine, in Stat Hall, behind the statue of Clio. I'm on my way."

The woman was just so damned intriguing.

"OK," he heard himself say.

# Chapter 12

Clio, Greek muse of history, was depicted in marble in the old House chamber, high above the floor in what was once the public spectator's balcony. The House had met in this space for the first half of the nineteenth century, but now the room was essentially a museum filled with the statuary of mostly obscure, forgotten figures in American history.

Clio's foot rested on a gilded timepiece as she cast a watchful eye over the hall. She cradled a large tome, quill pen poised over its pages as if recording the proceedings below. Her presence was a reminder for all who served that their deeds and actions would decide the fate of the young nation and carry the weight of history.

Tom looked over Clio's shoulder to watch for Loretta. The floor was as crowded as a stockyard with herds of high school kids on tour. A guide earnestly recounted the story of John Quincy Adams, the ex-president who had come to Congress after leaving the White House and died right here in this chamber after a virulent debate on the issue of slavery. Schoolgirls in belly-baring midriffs chomped on wads of gum, affecting boredom. The boys tried to impress them by imitating the grandiose poses of the figures ringing the chamber, or, if that didn't get the ladies giggling, rapping the backs of their hands against each other's nut sacks.

"How's the view from up here?"

He didn't see her approach. She was in the shadows behind him, a gleam in her eye and a saucy smile on her lips.

"Hello, Tom. Thanks for coming," she said.

"How could I resist?" His voice came out low and throaty.

"Why are you looking at my financial records?"

All business. Tom was immediately on defense. "I'm a reporter. It's what I do."

"It's what you're supposed to do. There are four hundred thirty-five of us. You have never in your life been down to the LRC, and one day you walk in out of the blue and ask for my records, and mine alone? I didn't just blow in off the prairie."

*For crying out loud,* Tom thought. *This place has more bugs than the Russian embassy.*

"What have they told you?" Loretta pressed.

"What has who told me?"

"Please, Tom. You know who. Dickey and that sad little lap-dog he keeps on a leash."

Apparently she knew plenty. "It's funny, Congresswoman. After seeing you with a spoon on your head the other day playing kissy-face with those two gentlemen you just mentioned, I would have thought you guys were tight buddies."

"Please answer the question."

"I'm the reporter. I ask the questions."

She welcomed Tom's insolence. *So Dickey thought he could use this cocky little bantamweight to bring me down? Guys like Salta were a dime a dozen around this town. So full of themselves. Cooing instead of speaking to me in a manner appropriate for addressing a member of Congress. All of these slimeballs—Dickey, Salta, that unspeakable shit Stu—were going to have to be taught a lesson in respect.*

"Of course you are," she said. "You looked at my records, and so therefore I'm sure you now have questions. So here I am. Go ahead and ask."

Tom usually enjoyed the role of impertinent reporter, but Loretta had a vibe that disarmed his instinct for confrontation.

He found himself suddenly fighting the urge to be chummy. To compensate, he conjured images designed to rouse his indignation and excite his journalistic ardor. He pictured all the members—especially this one—who were so used to people falling all over them, so used to getting whatever they wanted from whomever they pleased. But he was a network television correspondent, and he could say yes or no to putting them on national TV. They ought to be crawling over broken glass for the chance to be his friend, because he could be the one to make them big-time players just by granting them the exposure that they craved. *He could do that!* He wasn't just another toady, eager to offer her tribute—along with his professional virtue—for the privilege of tasting the breeze when she tousled her hair from one shoulder to the other.

His internal head game did the trick. "Why should I tell you what they said?" Tom shouted. "You don't have a right to the contents of my brain!"

Men had a tendency to behave oddly around Loretta. Once that started, it was only a matter of time before she got her way. Tom's anger was the tell, her cue to take control.

She stepped forward until she was inches from his chest, bit her bottom lip, tilted her head, and looked directly up into his eyes.

"OK, OK. You win, Tom. It's just that I think I know what they told you and what they're trying to peddle. All I'm asking is that before you buy into their slander and cheap smears and rush something onto the air, we talk about what is really at stake here and what I can do for you if you would just agree to be fair."

"I don't think so, Congresswoman." He retreated two steps, backing into Clio. "And please respect my space. I'm not some withered-up subcommittee hack. I don't come that easy." The words came out sounding like he was auditioning for the role of hard-assed journalist, but there was no depth to his performance. He had a funny feeling in his stomach. She was truly a force of nature. Stu was right to be worried.

Loretta affected a pout. "I forgive you for that, considering the people you have been talking to about me. I'm sure they've made me out to be the worst kind of strumpet."

"That's not—"

"And you're handsome and famous and I'm sure women come on to you all the time."

"Well, I—"

"See? I knew it. So I'm not offended if you jump to the wrong conclusions. But I'm not that kind of congresswoman."

"You're not?"

"Of course not! All I'm asking is that before you tell any more people about what you're working on, you come and talk to me first."

Tom tried to gather himself. "You will have ample opportunity to respond. You have my promise."

"Good. That's what I was hoping you would say." They shook hands and Tom felt a jolt shoot up his arm and down into his stomach. A thought suddenly came to his addled mind. "Oh, Congresswoman?" he called to the back of her head.

She turned, generating a luminous tsunami of hair that rose up from one shoulder and crashed down on the other. "Yes?"

"Can I have an interview later on the SUV thing?"

She smiled in satisfaction. "Of course, Tom. Come by at two?"

"Two," he mumbled. "I'll be there."

# Chapter 13

*It is a lonely life a man leads, who becomes aware of*
*truths before their time.*

—*Thomas Brackett Reed, Speaker of the House,*
*1889–1891, 1895–1899*

The woman on the subway was annoyed. Across the aisle a man appeared to be in some kind of trance, leering salaciously in her direction. Once about every other stop he reached down to adjust himself, digging into his crotch without embarrassment or regard for the car full of strangers who, as was customary on the Washington Metro, hurtled through the dark in colorless silence.

She couldn't have known that Tom's eyes, though unblinking and fixed in her direction, had no focus other than the ephemeral vision of Congresswoman Polk, the same image that had kept him tossing in bed all night. His mind was numb, and lack of sleep always left him as horny as a seminarian. The erection he absently fingered was pretty much the same one he'd been nursing for the last ten hours.

He was the unwitting central player in some great conspiracy. Was he right to be paranoid? Stu had known all about his caper with Billy at the Legislative Reporting Center, probably minutes after it happened. Loretta knew he had gone there in a hunt for her records. Dickey chose him for this story in the first place, knowing Tom's barren career prospects were fertile ground for his plot to destroy her. His swagger was gone. He was supposed to be the big-shot network correspondent, avatar of truth and keeper of the First Amendment flame. He wasn't clear on how he had become a witless pawn in the schemes of politicians.

He rode on, overcome with self-doubt and fatigue, the hobgoblins of a suppressed libido. He missed his stop at Union Station, only emerging from his dream state when the train clattered up a rise and into the bright morning sunshine, bearing north and away from the Hill.

At the Capitol entrance an overweight tourist set off the metal detector five times before he realized his belt buckle had to come off. On a normal day Tom would have said something snarky. He hated all the security. It cost him six or seven minutes on a bad day, waiting behind heartland types with their bladder bags and Main Street sensibilities, trying to cope with what everyone in Washington had taken for granted since the day after 9/11: the metal detectors, the roadblocks, bollards, the unmarked blimps hovering mysteriously overhead. To Tom it was all so unnecessary. Who would want to attack these guys in Congress? If they were really worth slaughtering, he'd get on the air much more.

He walked into the gallery, past Gil—already at his desk and fumbling with his computer—and on toward his booth, where he found a visitor in his chair for the second day in a row.

"Hey, pal," said Billy, lounging with his customary insouciance.

Billy hadn't dared show his face yesterday after the SUV spot had mysteriously appeared on BOP. There was no doubt Loretta was the source of the story, a fact that Tom found inexplicable. It wasn't like Billy could have charmed it out of her. Most members weren't Billy fans, owing to his pugnacious style and repugnant hygiene.

Clearly, she'd traded the General Accountability Office report for a favor, most likely some intel on what the two of them were really up to in the Legislative Reporting Center that day.

"What gives, man?" Tom pinched his fingertips together and gestured like his Italian grandfather. "You run an SUV story all day, and I get no heads-up, no love?"

"Sorry, man. I just thought you were so wrapped up in that other thing that you wouldn't have cared."

Tom eyed him suspiciously. "What, you mean she just calls you up and drops this stuff in your lap?"

"Something like that, yeah."

"Come on."

"What? It's not like you didn't get on the air last night. Damn nice spot, too. So stop ragging on me. You should be happy."

New York had given Tom a minute thirty to do the SUV story, and he'd barely had to lift a finger. A production assistant in the bureau had done the research. A producer had arranged and conducted three interviews, from which two sound bites totaling exactly thirteen seconds were lifted. The graphics people got a copy of the GAO report and whipped up some fancy effects. A script doctor in New York took Tom's bare-bones outline and punched it up.

Tom read the script into a microphone, and an editor, tapping the network's vast body of SUV file footage, assembled all the video and audio elements together into a tight package. Then Tom and his cheekbones stood in front of the camera, where he remembered to tilt his head a couple of times and employ just the right inflection at just the right moment as he recorded his stand-up. The editor tacked it onto the end of the spot, and bada bing, bada boom, Tom's mother had another keepsake for her cedar chest.

"So do you want to get some coffee before Dickey?" Billy asked. Today was the day for the majority leader's presser, due to start in ten minutes.

Before he could answer, the House bells began to ring.

"Oh, shit!" Tom looked at his watch, made two little jumps up and down, then threw his go-bag down on the desk in front of Billy and ran for the gallery door. "Got to make a pickup!" he yelled over his shoulder.

Billy watched the bag crash into the computer keyboard and slowly slide to the floor. He looked up to see Tom sprint from the gallery.

"Poor dumb bastard," he said aloud to no one.

# CHAPTER 14

Tom bounded down the grand marble staircase to the second floor. He passed under Clio and into Statuary Hall, fighting his way through a sweltering horde of Future Farmers suffering in their blue corduroy uniforms amid the heat of a Washington summer.

The clock stood in an ornate hallway just outside the Senate chamber. Capitol lore held that Senators used the cabinet in its belly to stash their booze during Prohibition. It was the kind of hokey pseudohistory that kept the teenaged tourists from yawning.

Tom bent forward and was running his hand over the clock's intricate millwork, feeling for the latch, when he sensed a figure approach from behind.

"Thinking of having a little eye-opener, huh?"

Tom jerked around to find a Capitol cop, an old-timer who had patrolled these halls for years. A friendly type and a celebrity at the family Thanksgiving table owing to the many famous senators and television news stars he had known during his thirty-four years on the force.

"I was thinking maybe a shot of schnapps to start my day," said Tom, playing along.

"Reminds me of the time Mondale came through here back in '79," the cop started in. "Of course, he was vice president at the time, as you know. He was also a senator, but before he was vice president." He folded his arms and rocked back on his heels. It looked like he was settling in for a long one. "Of course, the vice president is also the president of the Senate."

"Is that so?" Tom was prepared to feign interest for as long as it took to get rid of the guy.

"From Minnesota." The officer punctuated this information with a glance over the top of his eyeglasses. "Anyway, he walks by this clock, see, on his way to meet the majority leader. Well, of course I'm standing here on my best behavior, minding my own business, when he turns to me and says, 'I'll be back through here after this meeting, and I believe I might need a shot of whatever you've got in there today!' Like I had a stash of booze in the clock!"

"You're kidding," Tom managed.

"God's honest truth," said the cop.

"Wasn't his nickname Franz?" Tom asked, unable to help himself.

"Fritz," the cop quickly corrected.

The officer walked on shaking his head. *"Franz," the TV guy said. All that money they pay these guys, and they're nothing but idiots. This was going to make for a great story at lineup.*

Now the coast was clear, so Tom kneeled again before the clock and quickly found the cabinet latch. He pulled it open and peered inside.

Nothing.

He reached in and blindly ran his hands to every corner. Still no docs. He put his head halfway in and looked some more. Hollow.

Stu must have forgotten. Tom started back through the Capitol for Dickey's office at a sprint. He took a sharp left in the middle of Statuary Hall and ran through a door into the majority leader's suite, bursting in just as Dickey was stepping before the cameras. Reporters looked up and smiled, welcoming the promise of another outburst to rescue them from the tedious monotony of the leader's weekly briefing.

Tom found Stu in the behind the row of cameras. He urgently motioned for him to come into the foyer.

"Are you all right?" Stu asked once the pair was clear of the room. "You don't really look like yourself."

"The docs aren't in the clock," Tom said breathlessly. "Tell me you changed your mind and they're sitting on my desk in the gallery."

"What do you mean?"

"I mean the docs aren't there in the goddamn clock like you said they'd be!"

Some turn pale when they hear something shocking, but not Stu. He couldn't get any paler than he already was. But Tom could tell he wasn't taking the news well when he started blinking uncontrollably.

Stu turned to a young staffer. "Get me that page. The one with the hair," he barked.

He turned back to face Tom. "I'd stay away from Dickey today if I were you."

"Why? You haven't told him about our arrangement with the documents, have you?"

"No, I have not. He's pissed about the latest BOP story."

A chill ran down Tom's back. "What BOP story?"

"The BOP story about the pork barrel project that Dickey had stuck into the appropriations omnibus. Moving an NOAA division to Tennessee. It's a blind source, but we're pretty sure we know where it came from."

"Where?" Tom asked, as if he didn't already know the answer.

"Where do you think?"

It just didn't add up. How could Loretta still be feeding BOP stories, Tom wondered, especially after he had agreed to meet and assured her that he would give her a chance to rebut the charges? Jesus! Billy was kicking his ass.

"But Loretta isn't even on appropriations," Tom said lamely. He was in denial about Billy's betrayal.

"Let's just say that she has some fans on that committee," Stu said.

*Like the horny goat at Chowder and Marching,* Tom thought.

"Dickey was speculating about the best way to motivate you on the other thing," Stu continued. "He expressed the belief that a cowboy boot up past your sphincter might do the trick."

A page appeared. He wore a blue blazer with gray flannel pants, the page dress code. But a spray-painted blue streak from the nape of his neck up and over the top of his head and down to his bangs gave him away as a nonconformist. Dickey's staff didn't like it, but they checked the House manual and were unable to come up with a rule against multicolored hairdos on pages.

Stu pulled him aside and began to whisper urgently. "I swear it," Tom heard the page say.

"He swears he left it there," Stu reported back to Tom a moment later. "Are you absolutely sure you looked in the right place?"

"Oh, Jesus Christ, Stu! How could you have let me talk you into this stupid thing with the clock! Just tell me you have copies!"

Stu hesitated. "Of course I have copies. But it isn't that easy."

"Can I just wait here until you go get me another set?"

Stu's eyelids throbbed. "Salta, you are a lazy, selfish man!" he yelped. Several people in the presser turned to look out in the hall.

"What did I say?" asked Tom.

Stu threw up his hands and stormed back in. A scribe was in the middle of a question about the agriculture reauthorization bill. "Thank you!" Stu shouted, interrupting. "That concludes this week's press conference!"

Confused reporters shuffled out. Billy gave Tom a smile as he walked past. Tom responded with a raised middle finger, mouthing, "Eat me."

Another young staffer appeared at his elbow. "Mr. Albertson says he has the package you have requested. If you'll just step this way," she said. She gestured toward the door of the copy room.

Tom eagerly stepped forward. But when the door swung open, there was Dickey himself. Stu was on the other side of the room and looking like he'd just wet his pants.

"You know, Tom, I think coverage of the House should be mandatory for all reporters. Two-year conscription, minimum," Dickey began. "That way maybe all you fancy folks could begin to understand the people who send us here to run the place. Who voted to make us the majority. What do you think?"

Tom wasn't sure if he was supposed to respond.

"Under ordinary circumstances I would have planted that pork story myself." Dickey went on. He sat atop the copier, sporting his usual maniacal grin. Always in control. Always on. Never showing anger, never venting. Still, there was no handshake for Tom this time.

Dickey turned his chin slightly in Stu's direction. "Stu, I ever tell you about the time we sent a hundred million dollars down home for that naval lab?"

"Yes, sir," Stu stammered. Tom guessed that he had heard it about a hundred and fifty times, minimum.

"Hell, there ain't blue water within six hundred miles of where we got that thing put in." Dickey chuckled. "But damn if it didn't bring a two hundred jobs to our little county. One of the papers up here wrote up an editorial. Called me 'The King of Pork.' I blew that headline up so the letters were six feet tall, then put it on a billboard back home. Didn't I, Stu?"

"Sure did," Stu said in a small voice.

Dickey nodded thoughtfully and crossed his arms. "It's like my old daddy used to say: long as they spell my name right, I don't care what they say about me. 'Wear it like a badge of honor,' he'd say. 'Keep your enemies close and your friends at arm's length,' he'd say."

"At arm's length," Stu echoed.

"These fellas today. The Tea Party. All of a sudden 'pork' is a dirty word. It's like they're all kosher." Dickey chuckled to himself, savoring his moment of improv. "What they don't understand is this whole place is designed to divvy up the fruits of prosperity. But in times of lean, when the fruit don't come, well, that's when people get mad."

Dickey dismounted the copier and started to pace. "Here's the thing, Tom, and it kills me to admit it," he allowed. "All of a sudden I have to care about what the papers are writing about me. I can't be seen as just another local pol bringing home the bacon. I'm on the national stage now, son."

Tom was confused. "Mr. Leader, I think you may be mistaken. Neither I nor my network aired that pork story."

Dickey came to a stop. "But somebody did, Tom. Somebody did." His tone was ominous. "And here's the thing that upsets me: I thought I had the power to control these kinds of things. As a matter of fact, I was under the impression that I had taken steps to exercise that power back when we made our little arrangement."

Tom felt like he was far up the Mekong and face to face with Colonel Kurtz in *Apocalypse Now.* "I see," he said. He glanced at Stu, who at that moment was as wild-eyed as Dennis Hopper. "Well, Stu and I have talked about some of the issues surrounding that story, and I think you'll find that everything is going to work out fine."

Stu was behind Dickey madly waving Tom off.

"Have you now?" Dickey craned his neck and looked for Stu. "This one never ceases to amaze me," Dickey said of his trusty aide.

He paused as if struck with a thought. "By the way, you may not know that I've got one fixin' to leave the nest."

Tom was again off balance. Dickey never talked openly about his family. From what Tom remembered from a boiler-plate website bio, he had a daughter who had once been married but was now divorced. It took a moment before Tom caught on. "Stu?"

"Well, as a matter of fact, yes," Dickey said, oddly hesitant. "I suppose you could call him one of my own, the old hangdog. Just look at him. Don't look like he's got it in him, does it?"

They both turned to regard the sniveling wretch on the other side of the copier. It didn't seem possible that anyone would settle for him as a husband.

Intrigue, treachery, betrayal, and now the melodrama of an improbable romance. Tom imagined himself a spear-carrier in an Italian opera. It almost required surtitles. "We *are* talking about an actual female, yes?" Tom asked. "A human female, I mean."

A moment's anger played across Dickey's face.

Stu cleared his throat. "Tom and I have talked it over, Mr. Leader, and we have come to an agreement," he began, changing the subject. "I think that Tom understands what we expect of him now."

Both Dickey and Tom looked expectantly at Stu.

"We have agreed that Tom will contact me personally each day with a report on his progress," Stu said in a voice laced with malevolence. "Right, Tom?"

"Right." Tom played along. There were no odds in arguing with crazy people.

"Well then, that is excellent news," Dickey said. "And what progress can you report today?"

"Today? Well, today is just getting started."

"I see. And yesterday?" Dickey asked.

"OK. Come on now," Tom said, squirming. "You need to have a little patience. This is taking a little time, is all."

"Time," Dickey repeated flatly. "That is something that is limited in this particular situation." His eyes narrowed. "I ain't going to wait on you much longer."

# CHAPTER 15

The air had cooled in the afternoon. A slight breeze brought the first taste of autumn across the Potomac, the kind of weather that triggered a jones for a nice pint of stout, creamy as butter and dark as molasses.

Tom stood outside on the House steps and tried to clear his head. He reasoned that it might be best to take a moment to think things over, and, as if on their own volition, his legs began to take him in the direction of the Hill pub crawl. Ten minutes later he was hooking a foot around a barstool in the Corinthian Lounge and ordering a Guinness.

The place was empty. Just Tom and his pal Janine, the bartender, who at that moment stood atop a beer cooler reaching for a burned-out bulb in a lamp above the bar. She was young, and she had a classic kind of sensuality, like a Modigliani odalisque—only slightly more clothed. She stretched for the light without shame, her mons mere inches from Tom's face. Two fabulous melons were doing battle unfettered beneath the light cotton fabric of her top. You could bounce a dime off her tummy. In the small of her back she sported an extravagant sunburst tattoo, bracketed by the string of her skivvies, which grew as two tendrils from the top of her low-cut jeans and shot up and around either hip, joining together to plunge as one down into the glorious crack of her buttocks.

Tom stared, glassy eyed and mouth agape. He had suppressed his desires so successfully and for so long that he had almost forgotten what a compelling force lust could be. He felt a sudden urge to reach out and cup her crotch in the palm of his hand. It was the second time that day his mind had been clouded with desire.

He had sworn off womanizing years ago after his rakishness had got him into one too many scrapes at the outset of his career. Whereas as a young, handsome man fresh out of college and newly arrived in a given TV market he would greedily and happily fall down with virtually any willing female, he had by now resolved to live a life of acetic self-discipline. For Tom, that meant one girlfriend at a time.

It was no mean feat. He discovered early on that a lot of remarkably attractive women were available to a recognizable TV newsman. Many went out of their way to be associated with him, to the extent that a few nights of insane monkey sex could be described as an association. As he moved to bigger jobs in bigger cities, he found that the larger the market, the more chronic the pattern. He never made any promises and tried to be as open as he could about his interests, which were largely limited to carnality. That seemed to be fine with his partners, most of whom shared his narcissism. When things got a little complicated, as they often did, he'd try and keep the lid on until space became available on the next rung of the career ladder, which was usually at least five hundred miles away.

It had all worked out fine until Wichita, when the news director's wife helped herself to a handful of Tom one night in an edit suite during the eleven o'clock newscast. She'd been hanging around the station for weeks, showing up at odd hours on the pretense of coordinating the Christmas canned-food drive, which was inconsistent with the fact that she always arrived after regular business hours and was usually wrapped so tight in leopard-print Spandex it was a scandal just to look at her. That, plus the fact that it was the middle of May, made her intentions clear when she floated in night after night on a cloud of perfume and pinot grigio.

The whole newsroom knew why she was there. Everyone, that is, save the news director himself. He was a harried type, ensconced in his glass-walled office with the door closed for thirteen hours a day. There he was on the phone; here he was running a razor over his face; there he was meeting with the network affiliate liaison; here he was loosening his tie and, finally, needing another shave at the end of the day.

For the staff out in the newsroom it was like watching a pet hamster spin endlessly on its wheel. He was so immersed in the police blotter or the fortunes of the local sports teams that he scarcely noticed the day-to-day events happening in his own life that would never make the news. Yet they would conspire to destroy him if left unattended.

The guys over in the sports department were fans of Tom, a source of vicarious satisfaction. Fortunately for them, Tom wasn't stingy with the details of his prodigious sex life. It wasn't gentlemanly to kiss and tell, he knew. But he was a reporter, after all, and it was against his nature and training to keep secrets. After hearing him deliver another lewd account of his latest conquest, the sports guys would get real quiet and for the remainder of the night work with a single-minded focus, becoming exponentially more productive and turning out a very sharp sportscast. And after work, instead of heading across the street for a nightcap, they practically ran to their cars and raced home to their wives, whom they mounted with a ferocious intensity while they closed their eyes and pretended to be Tom Salta for a night.

Now, with the boss's wife so obviously on the prowl for their champion, Tom's jock buddies started a betting pool. The winner would be the one who correctly guessed the day that he finally had his way with her, or vice versa.

Even though he was still a reckless lad, Tom sensed trouble with this woman and tried to steer clear. She finally managed to get him alone in a deserted edit suite, where she made her play during—as fate would have it—the sports wrap-up segment. She pounced on him with a predatory quickness. Tom was overwhelmed at the raw sexual energy of this woman, who, after all, had a good twenty or so years on him. So he just sat back, closed his eyes, and allowed himself to be blown to a fare-thee-well.

"Throat yogurt!" exclaimed the weekend sports anchor, the winner of the pool, a mere twelve hours after the fact. By that time word had spread all over the newsroom, only bypassing the news director's glass prison.

Tom hadn't told a soul except the satellite truck operator, who gave him a lift home. They were friends who had shared a lot of personal anxieties on several late-night live shots, and Tom had sworn him to secrecy. So naturally, Tom was greeted the next morning with smirks and hearty backslaps from the sports guys, who had all the details. The women in the newsroom just shook their heads at him and kept walking.

A day or two went by, and Tom's loins swelled with a fresh supply of whatever it is that compels men to act as they do. So when she slipped him a note seeking to arrange a meeting—one where they could have a little more time and privacy "to experience the passion that occurs between two people who obviously care deeply for each other," he agreed to take an hour out of his day to disappear for a rendezvous at a hotel across town.

From there things got out of hand. They went at it like depraved animals in every conceivable position for hours at a time, less and less careful about the frequency and duration of their trysts. She was a dynamo. Tom was continually amazed at the depth of her desire and stamina. She began to bring him gifts and insist that they start spending more time together outside a hotel room. She framed her proposals to sound reasonable: Would it kill him if they went to go see a movie together? It was dark in a movie theater, after all. No one would notice. Or a drive in the country, someplace where nobody would know either of them? They could have lunch and go antiquing.

He wondered whether she was acting out a subconscious desire to get caught by her husband, either as a means to (finally) get his attention, or, more ominously, to destroy what was left of an unsatisfying marriage. That, or she really was becoming smitten with him. In any case, he figured it was time to start looking for the door.

As it turned out, he didn't have to worry about an exit strategy. The weekend sports guy—selfsame winner of the betting pool—had that covered when he went to the station manager and filled him in on his wife's salacious activities. Weekend Guy was a little sick of working weekends, and more than a little resentful of all the fuss over Tom, both within the network and all over town. His idea was to get points with the boss by telling him that his loving wife was really just a common slut.

"Thought you might like to know," he told the boss, "that Golden Boy was seen entering a motel out on the interstate with the missus." Being a Christian—and it being a Christian community—he felt that he was honor bound to tell the man, who by then had his face on the desk and his arms dangling toward the floor as he wept convulsively. The rest of the newsroom watched in silent pity from the other side of the glass.

Tom was fired, then blackballed around the country by the station manager, who had developed a far flung network of friends after twenty-six years in the business. It was six weeks of searching nationwide before Tom finally found work in Spokane. He was lucky he wasn't ruined for life.

Tom's eyes regained their focus on Janine's vulva, so graphically defined in the contours of her jeans. He had hoped his days of hitting on bartenders were over, but this was too much. He made a mental note to come back after he broke the Loretta story and sweep her away in the wave of his newfound fame. "Catch you next time, Janine the Dream," he said jauntily. He tossed a crisp twenty onto the bar and headed out the door.

A waitress appeared at Janine's elbow and offered a hit of her e-cigarette. "Jesus Christ. Is that guy living in his own world or what?" she said as they watched Tom standing outside, checking his phone. She pushed twin contrails of vapor through her nostrils. "I guess some guys just can't take a hint."

"No shit," Janine agreed. "I did everything but sit on his face."

# CHAPTER 16

There really was no use in going back to the Capitol, even though he should. It would be just his luck if something big broke—unlikely as that seemed—and he was caught at home, miles from his beat. He considered his options.

Then fate decided for him.

The blue-haired page was coming down Pennsylvania. The boy was clearly preoccupied—he didn't notice Tom standing there even as he narrowly missed walking into him. Tom watched as he turned sharply right and head down Second Street. A knapsack hung from his shoulder. Tom played a hunch and followed him.

He stayed well behind as the page moved quickly along sidewalks littered with softball pods of gingko seed. The pair moved south past turn-of-the-century row houses, their gardens of foxglove and sedum brimming through wrought iron fences with finials as sharp as spears. Every few steps the boy turned to glance over his shoulder, but he never saw Tom. When he reached the intersection that would lead him home to the page dormitory, he kept walking.

The page finally stopped at a grassy acre, hard by the elevated Southeast Freeway. An instructor was giving a lesson to a lone pupil on a vast tennis court. There was a playground, empty by now, the usual battalion of toddlers trundled home by their nannies. Once every thirty seconds or so a big semitrailer screamed by on the expressway.

As Tom stayed hidden he heard the grinding of a car's gears echo against the brownstones. He turned to see a white Jeep with its top down accelerating through an intersection two blocks back up Second Street. The glare of the afternoon sun against the windshield obscured the driver's face. The only clue to her identity was a whirl of ginger hair whipped like the flames of a wildfire in the wind of the open car.

"Bingo," Tom said to himself. He stepped back into the shadows as Loretta came to a screeching halt.

She got out of the Jeep, and as she approached the page suddenly leapt to his feet, like a vassal showing deference to a queen. She mussed his hair. "You're not going to regret this," she said, twirling a tress between two fingers. "You have made a very mature decision, and you will be rewarded."

Tom crouched like a commando and waited for the next semitrailer on the highway to cover the sound of his advance. He sprinted to a spot behind the bushes not six feet away.

The boy dug into his knapsack and produced a sheaf of papers bound with a big black clip. He handed them over, and as she glanced at the pages, Loretta said, "Come by the cloakroom next week?" She patted him twice rapidly on the thigh with her open hand and stood to leave.

The page again leapt to his feet, this time throwing his arms around her. Loretta gave him another tentative hug in return and threw in a few more strokes along his purpled locks. Several more seconds passed with his face buried in her bosom.

"Paul?" she said gently. "Paul, you have to let go now."

"But I'm so worried about you," the page said, his whimpering muffled in her cleavage.

"That's why I need to know if I can keep counting on you," she said.

He looked up at her suddenly, his face soaked in tears. "I won't let them do anything to you!" he wailed. "I'll do anything to stop them! Those bastards!" His arms fell from around her back, but his hands were now clenched in fists.

"My hero." She stroked his cheek with her knuckles, then lifted his chin. "You've already done so much. You're going to go far in this town—I'll see to it myself."

"But I don't care about any of that!" He was young enough to actually mean it.

# Chapter 17

Towering, black-bottomed storm heads encroached in the western sky, blotting out the late afternoon sun. At the first rumble of thunder Loretta ran for her car and wrestled with the soft top, trying to snap it into place to shield against a late-summer deluge. Tom made his escape just as big dollops began to splatter the sidewalk.

The Metro was eight blocks away. Tom would normally get an Uber, but he had been banned after several altercations with drivers. So he ran through the downpour back to Pennsylvania and aced out a middle-aged woman with her hand in the air to flag down a cab.

The foundation powder he habitually applied to his face each morning was now dripping onto the lapels of his $500 blazer. He sat on the cab's filthy vinyl seat as it crept along in rush hour traffic, only making it a block before coming to a dead stop in the gridlock. They had turned left and headed back down toward the freeway in the hope of finding a detour, when the cab jerked to a sudden halt.

"Son of a whore!" the cabbie shouted as he slammed on the brakes. "Would you look at this stupid bitch?"

They had narrowly avoided a collision with a white Jeep that had flat out run a stop sign. The cabbie lay on the horn and let out a stream of invective in a language that Tom didn't recognize, which somehow made it seem even more vulgar than it doubtlessly was.

"Follow her," Tom calmly told the driver.

"Look, mister, this is not such a big deal," the man said. "There are the crazy assholes all over the place. If we fight every time one does something stupid, then we never stop the fighting!"

"Follow her!" Tom barked. Loretta was heading south, beyond the freeway, where there was nothing but derelict warehouses and seedy strip bars.

"I don't want no trouble, mister," the cabbie mumbled.

"Please, it's not what you think," Tom said. "I hate to tell you this, but the woman in that car is a friend of mine. I mean her no harm, I can assure you. Now will you please just follow the Jeep?"

The cabbie's coarse bravado returned. "You know this bitch?"

"Yes, and I intend to give her a good talking to about her terrible driving. But I can only do it if you go up there and take a left on New Jersey. OK?"

The cabbie mumbled an ancient curse. Yet he did as he was told and pointed his cab west. "Still going to have to charge you for a Chevy Chase run," he said.

They passed under the freeway and entered a parallel universe of dilapidated buildings and broken glass, the curb littered with abandoned vehicles long disemboweled. The gutter ran a greenish black with the grimy effluent of their bushings and rusted radiators, forming a confluence with the rain bound for the Anacostia. Tom looked out at the wretched landscape and wondered what in the hell Loretta could be doing down here in this no-man's land. He'd seen nicer slums in Port-au-Prince. It was all just blocks from the Capitol's marbled corridors.

"Hold it!" he yelled, but the cabbie had seen it too and was already bringing the taxi to another screeching halt. It was the Jeep, pulled over half a block down a cross street in front of an old warehouse. The cabbie turned down the block and eased in behind a rusting hulk twenty yards away.

The brake lights went dim as the Jeep door opened. A long, tanned leg stretched from the driver's side, bridging the rank gutter. A blue umbrella unfolded into the rainy sky, and out popped Loretta.

Fanciful cursive reading "Fester's" was fashioned in neon and hung on an awning at the warehouse entrance. A hulking man with multiple piercings and a tight black T-shirt was stationed below, his bald head colorfully inked. He brightened at the sight of Loretta.

"Hi, Scotty!" Loretta said happily as she breezed past.

"Sue-weeeeet Loretta," the man replied, grinning broadly. He slid off his stool and bowed theatrically.

Tom threw forty dollars onto the seat next to the cabbie and jumped out onto the crumbling sidewalk.

"Hi, Scotty!" Tom said, mimicking Loretta, and made for the entrance without breaking stride.

"Hold on a second there, my man," Scotty said. Conservatively dressed guys showing up on ladies' night with beer on their breath were a constant concern. Especially the ones wearing makeup. The doorman looked at Tom and saw a typically confused, white-collar, bicurious straight guy who had worked up the nerve to come to Fester's, the premier gay dance club in the city. Guys like this usually had a wife and kids in Herndon, who right about now were just sitting down to dinner while Dad was supposedly working late at the office. Either that or he was a closeted gay man with the same wife and kids who just didn't know that tonight was ladies' night, in which case Scotty would be more sympathetic.

"Do I know you?" he asked Tom.

"Well, you might," Tom replied, tilting his head and smiling broadly. People were always approaching in vague familiarity. Part of the deal when you were on TV. There were times when it came in handy. "Would you like an autograph?" he asked enigmatically.

"That won't be necessary," Scotty replied. "Why don't you just go on in, Mary? I have a feeling that you might be disappointed, but go on ahead."

Tom pointed at Scotty with an index finger and pulled the trigger on an imaginary pistol. "Right-o," he said, and he sauntered in.

The club was a vast, dark cavern, the very walls redolent of cologne and clove cigarettes. Speakers the size of delivery trucks bounced a syncopated beat of house music against Tom's breastbone. A long bar ran along one side of the dance floor, which was big enough to land Marine One. Tom could make out the silhouettes of about a dozen people in the hazy gloom. A few dancers were visible for split seconds at a time, freeze-frames captured in a strobe.

Tom entered a smaller side room and scanned halfway down a row of booths before he spotted Loretta seated with her back to him, her silhouette unmistakable even from behind. A woman in a bob haircut and a conservative suit sat with her, waving a cigarette around like a flare in the dark as she gestured between drags. She inhaled fiercely, and Loretta nodded along as the woman became more and more animated.

"We cannot go public!" Tom thought he heard the woman tell Loretta over the noise. "We can still get him to stop!"

The woman continued with her sternness and her smoking, and soon Loretta's shoulders began to heave. She hid her face in her hands. The woman stopped her harangue and gently held Loretta's wrist. But that only brought more sobbing and heaving. Finally, she grabbed Loretta by the arm and dragged her out of the booth.

They were coming right for him. Tom ducked under a staircase just before Loretta was pulled past. They hadn't seen him. He had made it just in time.

"Do you fucking mind?" A voice came out of the darkness from a point very close.

Tom jumped back a step. He held up his cell phone, and its beacon illuminated two women in an embrace.

"What the fuck are you doing here, asshole?" one of them growled, squinting into the light. "Are you some kind of sick twist?"

"I'm terribly sorry," he stammered as he fled.

"Fucking breeder!" the shorter woman spat out after him.

"Sick fucker!" the other hollered into the din.

Tom took refuge at the far end of the bar by the dance floor. He was only blocks from the Capitol, where people paid tribute to him, the all-powerful network man, when they passed in the corridors. Six blocks away and he was completely out of his element. He started to wonder if he was really that out of touch. Was his reality just Washington make-believe? The rest of the population spoke a different language, playing out the drama of their lives under darkened staircases or in smoky bars, on tennis courts or in places like Dickey's district back in Tennessee. People didn't care about the dreary world of politics and media that he had spent the last four years trying to conquer. No one here gave a shit who he thought he was. One trip outside the Capitol's cloistered halls and he was lost.

"What'll it be, Mary?" asked the bartender.

*What a fool I am*, he thought. *It took twenty minutes of being referred to as "Mary" in a room full of lesbians to realize that I'm in a gay bar. Some reporter.*

"I said, what are you having?" the bartender repeated, more firmly now.

He was suddenly self-conscious. *Everyone in this place is gay,* he thought, *and I'm sitting here sticking out like a porn star's boner.*

"Last chance, man." The bartender was tired of being ignored. "You can't sit here and not drink."

A syllogism started to form in his head: *If this is a gay bar, and everyone in here is a woman who is either making out with another woman or looking to be making out with another woman, and Loretta is here with another woman, therefore…what does that make Loretta?*

He finally took notice of the bartender, who was still standing in front of him, annoyed. "This is a gay bar, isn't it?" he shouted over the music.

"You're a fucking genius!" she shouted back.

He turned his back on her and found Loretta on the dance floor. Only she wasn't dancing. She stood stock still with her head down as the friend gyrated around her, moving closer with each orbit. The friend stretched her neck and tilted her head from side to side as she took tiny steps, looking like a flamingo in mating season. The strobes captured her in a seductive series of poses: first in front of Loretta with her hands in the air, a split-second later on tip toe with her pelvis thrust forward. The third flash revealed her stroking Loretta's hips from behind, then tousling her hair, now beside her and humping her leg, then pressing her breasts to Loretta's. A final rapid-fire series of bursts revealed the two women in each other's arms, their mouths locked in a passionate kiss. Tom could hardly believe what he was seeing.

He felt a hand grip the top of his shoulder and he turned to see Scotty, flanked on one side by the two women from under the stairs and on the other by the bartender.

"That's him! That's the pervert who wanted a three-way under the staircase!" cried the short woman in the tank top.

"Yeah. And then he thought he could sit here and get his rocks off free of charge and not order a drink," the bartender chimed in.

"Now hold on just a second here." Tom slid off the barstool and began to explain, "I'm not what you—"

"He's got a hard-on!" exclaimed the second woman from under the stairs. She was urgently pointing in the direction of Tom's crotch.

Tom looked down at his tumescence, then up at Scotty.

"Your choice," Scotty said, "through the door or out the window."

Tom stood in his soaking-wet clothes, mottled face, and withering erection. He had no words. Moments later he was hurtling back through the front door and out into the damp night, propelled all the way to the rank gutter, where he landed with a splash.

"And stay out!" Scotty shouted after him. His three accusers howled with laughter from under the awning.

# Chapter 18

*Political language... is designed to make lies sound truthful and murder respectable, and to give an appearance of solidity to pure wind.*

—*George Orwell*

There are stages to a catharsis. A lifetime of anger can't be flushed away in one sitting and three bottles of wine. Reversion to the mean is the easy path. Muscle memory impelling one foot to go before the other. Nibble at your pain like comfort food and you're malnourished, but at least still alive. Crawl and hide inside the welter of scars and calloused earned over years of battering neglect. Turtle up when things get tough. It's hollow in there. Plenty of room in the space where your soul should be.

Cornelia's life changed on the day of her meeting with Loretta over wine in Adams Morgan. She held nothing back, listing the counts of her indictment like a bailiff: Her father was worse than selfish. He treated her as a commodity to be traded, a chit in his constant maneuvering for power. She had no control over who she was and what would become of her, and she never had.

Loretta counseled the younger woman to stand up and step out from under her father's grinding heel. "Be happy," she told her. "Seize this chance. Maybe your last chance."

Loretta had been there with her own father. And her husband. She was a young woman out on the high plains, and there was no one to turn to and everyone to turn to, because virtually every woman she knew had gone through it. They understood. It's just that they didn't care. To their way of thinking, Loretta's problems weren't special and neither was she. They had dealt with it and so would Loretta. Loretta hated that her husband considered her to be some sort of walking lifetime achievement award. But when she rebelled, the sisterhood turned on her, clawing at her legs like crabs in a bushel barrel, pulling her back into the suffocating pile just as she teetered on the edge of escape.

It was an ethos that scoffed at introspection. Life was all about duty and discipline. Loretta was hard that way, and bitter experience had left her the type of woman who never opened up to another woman. She had learned to go without that kind of friendship. But now all that had changed.

In the weeks that followed their Adams Morgan sit-down, each woman allowed the other to see what had always been too painful to reveal. To speak of it, to give it a name, to identify the subtle manipulations at the hands of the men in their lives that time and disappointment had finally exposed. Cornelia was in awe of Loretta, her spiritual guide. Together they opened veins for each other until their bodies ran free of the toxic poisons of a political life.

Loretta saw the danger of a backlash. Pockets of anger, hidden for years in Cornelia's marrow and lurking in her ganglia, were ripped open. The foundations of her identity were shifting, triggering a tide of angry resentment that was gaining strength. If Loretta wasn't careful it might roll right over her.

People complain about their spouse or lover or parent, teacher or coach or best friend. Oaths are sworn and feet put down. But offer more than a shoulder to cry on, offer to abet revenge, and the fire of vengeance may be trained on you, the interventionist. Abusive relationships work that way. There's a tipping point. Sometimes people just need to bitch. When push came to slap, Cornelia might defend her family.

But the stages of catharsis telescoped into one, and it wasn't long before Cornelia's anger gathered force until it was a class five hurricane heading straight for her father. Each conversation between Dickey and his daughter became more contentious. It took little more than two weeks before they weren't talking.

Cornelia's cooperation in the conspiracy against Minton was now out of the question.

Just as a salesman makes the easiest mark for a sales pitch, no one falls for the coercive talents of a politician like another politician. Zach Dickey was sold on Loretta in the very first moments of their introduction, sensing that she possessed an unusually strong power of persuasion, blessed as she was with looks and presence. From that moment on he worked hard to co-opt her. He could see that she would be either an invaluable ally or a fearsome enemy. So he brought her into his orbit.

But he didn't count on this: Cornelia and Loretta Jean Polk, aligning as two celestial bodies, together breaking free of his planetary pull. So as he sat before his computer on that first day of wine and tears, witnessing the live stream from the cop's phone in the Adams Morgan bistro and Loretta's embrace of his sobbing daughter, Dickey saw his judgment confirmed. This woman was dangerous. This was a manifest nightmare. It was time to take off the gloves.

He threatened Loretta's committee seat if she would not go after Minton. She had no reaction. He vowed to shut off her campaign-money spigot. She scoffed. He appealed to her sense of party loyalty. She cackled at him. He pulled all the usual levers, pushed all the usual buttons. She simply looked back at him with a silent, seething contempt.

He played his trump card. "If you won't do it for me, do it for your dear, late husband, who would be turning over in his grave if he knew that you were in league with our enemies." At this she slapped his face, turned, and walked out of his suite.

Cornelia knew she had entered a new level of recovery when she howled at news of the confrontation. She was shocked that she wasn't shocked. She asked Loretta for every detail. Did she hit him with an open hand or a closed fist? A right or a left? What was his reaction? Did his protective detail see any of this? They were entering an uncharted region in the dark psyche of Zach Dickey. There was no telling what kinds of monsters were lurking there.

# CHAPTER 19

The last several days, culminating in the confrontation at Fester's the night before, were beginning to take their toll on Tom. His breezy confidence had taken some hard hits since he came to DC, but this was different. This was an existential crisis. His abilities, his confidence, his charm...the foundations of his success were starting to crack, weakened by years of venality and feckless bullshit that—it was becoming brutally clear to him now—were the hallmarks of his career. For the first time he saw that it could all come crashing down.

Tom struggled with the ambiguous tangle of contradictions that was at his essence as a journalist. He knew he wanted fame, but he didn't want the scrutiny that came with it. He was quick witted, but he was shortsighted. He was intuitive about politics, but he lacked the discipline and desire to really dig deep. He had dreams of grandeur, always on the hunt for the one big scoop that would vault him over the top, but he wanted it wrapped in a bow and delivered to his doorstep. It wasn't that he was callow. He simply lacked the clawing ambition he needed if he was to get all the way to the top. He had come to the humbling point where he just wanted respect, to be liked by the people of his world. He craved acceptance, reassurance, and affirmation. The irony was that his newfound insecurity and thinning skin were traits that he shared with the public officials he so loathed.

Of course, the morning after Fester's the first person he would run into in the Capitol's basement cafeteria was Billy, the fucker. Tom's mouth foamed with spite for his former pal, which he ameliorated by informing Billy that his number one source and Washington's answer to Katy Perry was actually a lesbian.

"Now *that's* a scoop," he spat. "So how do you like me now, Judas?"

"Get the fuck out of here," said Billy. As far was he was concerned, this was the last act of a desperate man. *Coming up with some crazy story about Loretta being gay? Just pathetic. The guy gets beat on a couple of stories, and look at him. A wreck.* Billy skipped breakfast and left.

Tom wasn't sure what to do with this newfound information. There was still some limit to how low ABN would go. At this point the elastic standards of what made news had been grotesquely stretched, that was true. But the universe of acceptable behavior had also expanded. So Loretta Polk is gay. And? Only a small lost

colony of social conservatives would care. And they didn't watch
ABN. The people who did would only be indignant that this sort
of thing passed as news on the network. Maybe if there were some
pretense. If she were an outspoken homophobe, a backer of conversion therapy, or some other nonsense. Then he could righteous-
ly expose her hypocrisy. Sadly for Tom, that was not the case.

But there was another way he could make it work for him.
God knows that Stu and Dickey had a million nefarious uses for
a piece of intelligence like this. It would be pure dynamite in their
hands. And it would get them off his back for at least a week. He
dialed up Stu and arranged to meet him by Clio.

"What is it with you and the cloak-and-dagger stuff?" Stu
asked as he arrived at the top of the stairs behind the statue. The
climb had left him covered in a damp sheen.

"I have come bearing you a great gift," Tom solemnly
proclaimed.

"The story is on the air tonight?"

Tom made a wiping motion with his hand, as if swatting
away something small but bothersome. "We'll get to that," he
said. "Right now I have a bit of info regarding our congresswoman that you might find rather incredible, not to mention
scandalous."

Stu raised his eyebrows. "OK."

"This is going to blow your mind. I know it blew mine," Tom reported.

"On the scandal?" Stu seemed surprised.

"Oh, it's a scandal all right. No question about it."

Stu was puzzled. The Tom he knew was vapid and indolent. It didn't seem possible he could have found something on Loretta by himself. But as Dickey often said, even a blind squirrel finds an acorn every now and then.

"You must have finally read those docs that you stole from the LRC. Could it be that our big-shot reporter has finally come through with some real reporting on his own?"

"Uh, yeah," Tom hedged. "Let's just call it good field work."

"Excellent news, Tom!" Stu exclaimed. "And I, in return, have something for you as well, my sleuthing friend." He grandly produced a sheaf of papers. "The copies of the documents, as promised. Put these together with whatever it is that you have uncovered. I think you'll find it's an open and shut case." He handed them over with uncharacteristic joy. "It goes without saying that you didn't get this from me."

Tom bowed solemnly. Maybe things weren't so bad after all.

"So when can you turn this around? For tonight's show?" Stu asked.

Tom thought it would be possible to have it on air tonight—provided of course that the new documents were the real goods—but it would be a rush job. Anyway, he'd made his promise to Loretta, and he would honor it. He would give her a chance to respond. Twenty-four hours sounded like a reasonable deadline.

"I think to do the story right might take a day or so. I'm thinking tomorrow night, most likely," Tom told him.

"Fine!" Stu said gleefully. "I'll program the DVR as soon as I get home. Now, let's see the docs that you have come up with."

"It's not exactly documents. It's more like some intel that you and Dickey can no doubt find some way to employ for your diabolical purposes."

Stu's smile sagged a little at the corners. "What kind of intel?"

There's a part of many men that never left high school. The towel-snapping impulse to talk sex—exaggerating exploits, their own or others'—was a part of the locker room code they were compelled to disdain in public, but enjoyed in private. Tom was one of those guys. Stu was definitely not.

Tom moved closer. "Dig this, my man: she's a lesbian," he whispered.

One of Stu's eyelids suddenly twitched. The rest of him went rigid. "Who's a lesbian?"

"Hard to believe, isn't it? Capitol Hill's own beauty queen and all-American girl, a carpet muncher."

"I asked you a direct question," Stu said, too loudly. "Who are you talking about?"

"Who the fuck do you think? I'm talking about Loretta Jean, the lesbo machine."

Stu's eyelids began an arrhythmic throbbing. "What would make you say a thing like that?" he demanded.

"Check it out: I followed her down to this place in Southeast last night, on the other side of the freeway. I get inside and sit there like an idiot in the dark, but I finally realize I'm in a gay bar. Did you know about this place? It's called Fester's. It's only, like, five blocks from here."

Stu made a squeaking sound.

"Anyway, about the time that I figure out what the fuck is going on in this place, I look up and see our girl Loretta eating face with another chick right out on the dance floor."

"I think you must be mistaken," Stu croaked.

"I know it's hard to imagine, but try. I have to tell you it was one of the more titillating things I've ever seen. I didn't get much sleep last night. You feel me?"

"You are a vapid, sick man."

"That's the second time I've been called sick in the last twenty-four hours." Tom was almost proud.

Stu put a thumb to each eyelid and pushed down. "Who was the other woman?" he asked, though he didn't want to know the answer.

Tom looked at Stu and saw the product of a stilted, unhealthy outlook toward human sexuality, symptomatic of his subjugated soul. God only knew what his love life was like with this mystery fiancée of his. No wonder he was miserable.

"That's the weird part," Tom began. "You would think that a woman of Loretta's caliber would have her pick of every box biter in the country. But this babe was totally lacking flavor. Plain old bob haircut, knee-length skirt, pale complexion. Smoked like a fucking fiend. I'd rate her a six, maximum."

Stu's breathing became shallow and rapid.

"And to top it off she was mean as cat shit. Started screaming about how she wouldn't go public. That's all I could hear. She made Loretta cry."

Stu started swaying. He stumbled to the granite wall and leaned back.

"Jeez. Are you OK?" Tom took him by the arm. "I didn't think you were this much of a prude, for crying out loud. I thought you would be grateful for the intel."

Stu let his knees go slack and slid down, smearing a damp trail that tracked his descent. He wrapped his arms around his knees and began to sob.

# CHAPTER 20

*Remember, democracy never lasts long. It soon wastes,*
*exhausts, and murders itself. There is never a democracy*
*that did not commit suicide.*

*– John Adams*

Of course it had to be Minton. That was just the way Tom's life was working out lately.

Stu's documents laid it all out. First was a letter from a whistleblower within the ranks of Minton middle management. It alleged systemic fraud, deceit, and reckless disregard of regulatory requirements leading to wildly inflated quarterly profits and, as a result, the inevitable ripping off of thousands of investors. The letter clearly implicated the company's top management but was especially damning for Minton's CEO.

Next, there were transcripts of legal depositions from officials within Minton, wherein Loretta Jean Polk was accused of threatening the company with public disclosure of the whistleblower's charges of malfeasance, which she had access to as chairwoman of the full committee's subcommittee on investigations and oversight. The price for her silence on the matter was alleged to be $500,000 in cash, to be delivered on a thirty-eight-foot Hinckley yacht, both of which were to be transferred into her possession at a slip in the nearby Washington Marina.

Finally, there were copies of sell sheets from Loretta's online brokerage account that chronicled a series of orders to dump all the Minton stock in her portfolio. The date of the sales was the day after the whistleblower's letter had been date-stamped "RECEIVED" in committee offices.

Tom read the dossier, each and every page. When he was done, he tossed them all up onto his desk in a loose pile, sighed, and leaned back into his chair.

He had a decision to make. Going with the story would result in the utter destruction of his stock portfolio and—not that it really mattered to him at this point—possibly the entire ABN network that was a subsidiary of Minton and that also happened to be his employer. That was on the one hand.

On the other hand, did he have a choice? His entire career, all the guiding principles of this life as a journalist, led him to this moment. Speaking truth to power. Holding the feet of the powerful to the flame of accountability. The voice of the voiceless. The public's right to know. The ideals that once filled him with a righteous sense of mission. A cause to live for and a code to live by. Were they all just empty motivational slogans fit for printing on a tee shirt, and about as useful?

The easy way out would be to pitch it all into the white-paper recycling bin. Forget about the whole thing and go back to his life as a member of the club, finding affirmation in his reflection in the eyes of others who mistakenly believed he was a big deal. The sad irony would be that he had thrown away his chance to justify their reverence.

Was he really just an imposter? This was the reckoning, the time to confront the visceral fear that had hectored his conscience for years. If he walked away now, he would remove all doubt that he was nothing but a caricature of the shallow TV journalist.

He agonized, but only briefly. Soon, Tom found his backbone. It was time to take action.

He typed his username and password, accessing his brokerage account. Then he calmly rolled over all the Minton shares in his 401(k), transferring the lot of it into an IRA pegged to a nice, safe index fund.

He was going with the story, everything else be damned.

This was how things happened in the world. Fortunes were won and lost overnight. It would be old-fashioned, real breaking news, unadulterated and pure. A scoop to put him back on the network map, back on the path to stardom. He could be considered for promotion to the big chair. James Quinn, the legendary anchor of ABN's evening newscast, had held the throne for twenty-four years. He wasn't going to last forever.

Years of cynicism had left a residue of hard water stains coating the lining of his guts. The manipulation and the pandering. The race to the bottom to plunder the treasure chest of ratings. Perverting the primal human desire for information about the world around us with the sugar high of celebrity gossip and phony controversies.

At that moment Tom remembered what it was like to be righteous. He resolved to scour the impurities from his system. From *the* system.

# CHAPTER 21

*If you don't stand for something, you'll fall for anything.*

—*Irene Dunne*

The time had come to lay his cards on the table. Loretta's PAC office was just blocks north of the Capitol. He called her to set the meeting. He would go see her there to keep his promise and give her a chance to respond to the allegations before the story went on the air. It was only ethical. And it was due journalistic diligence.

Loretta had cheerily answered his call and told him to come over later in the afternoon. He spent an hour going over the documents one last time before setting out. As he rose floor by floor toward the confrontation that would define his career, he practiced his smile in the fun-house image of the elevator wall until he felt ridiculous. Did Bob Woodward primp like a sophomore on prom night before he went off to meet Deep Throat?

He got off on her floor and stood at her door, inert. Was it fear or self-doubt that wrapped around his spine like kudzu, short circuiting his neurons, blocking the hand from fulfilling the brain's command to knock? It was time to summon some discipline. And it was way past time to grow up.

He was still standing there when the door swung open. There stood Loretta, a hand on her hip and wearing the saucy grin that was becoming familiar to him.

"I'm sorry, young man, but we don't accept solicitations."

"May I come in?"

"My, my! So formal!" She wore a conservative shift of no particular distinction, loose fitting and—save for her bare arms—far less revealing than what he had witnessed at Chowder and Marching. He hurried past her, letting his go-bag slide off his shoulder and onto the floor.

It wasn't much of an office, more like a suite in one of the finer hotels around town, replete with wet bar, hand-woven Persian rugs, and a contemporary chaise lounge from Theodores. The main room was arranged for entertaining. A partition divided the space, and behind it Tom caught a glimpse of a large conference table.

"Would you like a drink?" She stood at the wet bar, shaking a bottle of vodka by the neck so the liquid splashed around inside. Tom feared that alcohol would weaken his resolve. On the other hand, it might just be the shot of courage he needed.

Loretta frowned. "Well, I'm not going to drink alone," she laughed. "Are you going on a trip someplace?"

"Uh, no."

"Such the conversationalist!" She put the bottle back on the bar. "I was just wondering about that big sack of yours over there," she said, gesturing to the spot on the floor next to Tom where he had dropped his go-bag.

They both regarded the bag. "This place is on my way home. I take the Metro."

"Oh, so you're green! Good for you!"

Tom was going for stoic.

"Oh for God's sake, Tommy. Why don't you sit down?" She gently put a hand around his bicep. "Just because you think you're here to give me bad news doesn't mean that we can't be friends, now does it?"

This would be the perfect time to draw the line. They were adversaries. Not friends.

"Congresswoman, I think I should tell you—"

"Please, call me Loretta." She was guiding him toward the couch.

The familiarity, the physical contact—subtle weapons in her vast array.

*Confidence*, he told himself. *Discipline.* "I think I'll have that drink, if it's still OK," Tom said.

"Well of course!" Loretta chirped. "Why don't you go on over and fix us up a couple? That is, if you don't mind me joining you."

Tom poured out two vodkas, making a mess of things with trembling hands.

"So I can call you Loretta Jean, instead of just plain ol' Loretta?" he asked, trying to regain his swagger.

"Well of course you can! Now why don't you just sit down and tell me all about what you have to tell me."

He'd rehearsed this presentation earlier in the afternoon, and hearing himself say it out loud beforehand convinced him even more that it was pretty much a slam dunk. It was all pretty straightforward.

He cleared his throat. "Well, Congresswoman—"

"Tom! Please! It's Loretta Jean to you. Now I mean that." She sat down next to him, showing not the slightest bit of fear, but gazing expectantly, a pleasant smile on her lips.

Her casual air was disconcerting. She had known virtually every move he had made over the past several days. He had no doubt that she understood the basics of the story, and that it could destroy her. But here he showed up at her door like the angel of death, and instead of desperation or anger, she was all sanguine and breezy. Flirty, even.

"Right. Loretta Jean." *God, she was awesome.*

"That's better."

"Anyway." He took a deep breath, pausing to summon a prosecutorial detachment. "I have come into possession of documents that indicate you have been using privileged information obtained in the course of your congressional committee duties to extort others and enrich yourself." He looked directly into her face. "And that, of course, is illegal."

"Eeew. That *is* serious, isn't it?" she said brightly.

"Is that all you have you have to say?"

Loretta put her glass down on the coffee table. "What is it that I should say, Tom? Should I beg you not to run the story? Should I throw a fit and curse Dickey and Stu? Get hysterical? What would you have me do?"

"So you're not denying these accusations?

"Of course I'm denying them. They're ridiculous."

"I should emphasize that I have documentation that backs it up."

Loretta sighed. "Tom, you're trying so hard to be a grown-up it almost breaks my heart, even though it's me you're trying to send to jail. You might think you want that, but you and I know that you really don't."

He was sorry that she had to be the one to go down, but he wasn't crazy about sitting here being treated like he was another foot soldier in her legion of admirers, no different than that purple-headed page boy. This was going too far.

"What about the documents?" Tom asked indignantly.

"They're fake."

"You haven't even seen them yet. How could you know that?"

"First of all, I don't need to see them to know they're fake, because what you just described has never happened."

*That's what they all say.* "I'm afraid that's not good enough."

"Second, you might think that I don't know what's in those bogus documents that those two clowns are trying to foist off on you, but I do."

*The rendezvous with Paul the page.* "I have looked them over myself. They look authentic to me."

Loretta smiled. "Did you every stop to think that Dickey and that pale limp-dick who follows him around everywhere were angry with me for something? And is there any doubt in your mind that they would stoop to any depths, including just plain old bald-faced lying and forgery, to get even? Like you said the other day, you're the reporter, you ask the questions. So did you ever ask those?"

*Well, yes to the first one and no to the second. Some things are too good to check.* "What makes you so sure that they're forgeries?"

"Now you're talking like a real reporter!" She rose from her seat on the couch and walked around to the other side of the partition. She returned holding a ream of paper.

"Why don't we just have a look together at the crap Stu is trying to peddle?" It was the package the page had handed over.

"Now, let's see," she said, thumbing through the documents. "Oh yes, here we are. This little item here is supposed to be a sell order that I placed on Minton stock a day after we learned of the whistleblower complaint, which I see Dickey and Stu have thoughtfully provided a copy of, as well."

Tom recognized these two documents as identical to those provided to him by Stu. It was damning evidence, no doubt. "So what's wrong with these? They look legit to me," Tom said.

"Tommy, Tommy, Tommy. This sell order is doctored!" She produced another document from a binder on the coffee table. "This is the real one." She handed it over to Tom. "Now check out the order number. It's the same as on the copy you have, right?"

Tom was quiet. He had no idea what the order number was on his version of the document.

"Oh, for God's sake," Loretta sighed. She got up and walked over to where Tom's bag lay on the floor and brought it over to the couch. She threw it down onto his lap. "Open it."

Tom did as he was told and zipped open the bag. He barely had the docs out before Loretta impatiently grabbed them from his hand.

"OK, here it is," she said, holding up the sell order. "See? The order numbers match. Everything on the heading, the salutation, right down to the blemish in the paper. They all match. Right?"

"Right."

"Now look at the dates. The original is dated exactly one year earlier to the day. All they did was change the last digit of the year. For heaven's sake, any bouncer in a College Park kiddie bar could have caught that on a fake ID."

Tom squinted close to the document. She was right.

"I sold every penny of that dog of a stock that day, a year before this supposed letter from this supposed whistleblower showed up," Loretta informed him. "I can assure you that it had everything to do with the fact I was losing thousands of dollars' worth of the value that my late husband had left me in Minton and nothing to do with any committee investigation."

The only thing keeping the floor from falling out beneath Tom's feet were the depositions. His last hope. If they were forged and he used them on the air, he would end up a laughingstock.

"There is another matter," he said, and pulled the depositions from his papers. "What about this?"

Loretta took them from his hand and began to read. For the first time since he arrived she wasn't smiling.

"Let me ask you something," she said finally. "Do you really think that this whole line of crap they are trying to sell you has anything to do with their sense of ethics and propriety?"

"Probably not," Tom admitted. On the other hand, if reporters started turning up their noses at every bit of information given to them by someone with a score to settle, then everyone's sources would dry up and Washington might was well disappear back into the swamp. "Nobody does anything for anyone around here for the sake of altruism. Their motivations are beside the point."

"It doesn't bother you that you're being used?" she asked.

It seemed like an esoteric question. "We all exploit each other, you know that. It's our bread and butter, yours and mine."

Loretta let out a scornful laugh. "Those who stand for nothing will fall for anything," she said.

"I don't see your point."

"Tom, I hate to break it to you, but Dickey didn't choose you as his bag man because of your skills as an investigative journalist. He knew you were desperate and wouldn't ask too many questions, for sure. But what you don't know is that this is all about his vendetta against the Minton CEO, your big boss. So the idea that a guy who actually worked for him would be the one to take him down was an extra twist of the knife he just couldn't resist."

At this point Tom was morose.

"Did Stu happen to mention that he was engaged to get married?" Loretta asked.

"Not exactly. Dickey was the one who brought it up, but he wasn't very clear on the whole thing."

"I guess not," Loretta said. "Don't ask me how I know, but it so happens that the woman that Stu thinks he's going to marry happens to be a Minton lobbyist. Both Stu and Dickey have access to her computer. And by virtue of the fact that they run the place, they have access to mine as well. They simply generated a fake letter from a pretend Minton-manager-turned-whistleblower using a Minton e-mail account. Then they altered a year-old sell order that I had made using my congressional Internet account. There is no way to describe these depositions, except that they are laughable. Nothing but a high school creative-writing exercise."

"So what are you saying? That these are forgeries too?" Tom asked meekly. He already knew the answer.

"Is there really any doubt in your mind?"

He wished he could melt into Loretta's couch and become one with the foam.

"Don't feel so bad." She stroked the back of his head. "You had the courage to come and confront me. Others wouldn't have bothered and would've run the story without even giving me the chance to set them straight. Imagine where you'd be if that happened."

Tom shrank from her like a puppy that had just been punished with a swat across the snout for peeing on the rug. He was shamed beyond humiliation. He suddenly saw that he was no investigative journalist. That was a fantasy, a movie role, and in his heart he had known all along that he didn't have the discipline, the fearlessness, or the desire to play it. He was way out of his depth. Who was he kidding? He was a TV guy. A good one, sure, as far as it goes. But the job description was inherently superficial. At bottom, Tom was motivated by a need for fame, inasmuch as fame carried affirmation from the world around him. But at that low moment he at last saw the essence of his self-delusion: he confused fame with respect, and respect is what he craved. He just wanted to be liked. By colleagues, by friends, by women, by the TV audience, and even by the public officials he was supposed to be holding accountable. But investigative journalists aren't liked, and to be one – a good one – you really can't care what people think of you.

Loretta had exposed him as a fraud, and it was all so effortless. He felt a strange gratitude. She was an extraordinary woman.

"May I use your bathroom?" he whimpered.

Kneeling with his face in the toilet, he waited for the convulsions that yielded only a teaspoon of brown, viscous fluid. He hauled himself up in front of the mirror and took a grim inventory. The first trace of crow's feet radiated from the corners of his eyes. Small moguls of fat were emerging along the clean slope of his jawline. Years of decaf and diet cola had dulled the gleam of his smile. The deepening black circles under his eyes evoked a thousand years of Calabrian forebears. He was proud of his heritage, but the hit-man look was not the thing for an anchorman. What was the use anymore in trying? It was only a matter of time before he would be cast off and forgotten. It was time to go home.

He walked out of the bathroom to find Loretta going through his bag.

"What do we have here?" She pulled out his gas mask, inspecting it like some futuristic artifact from an alien civilization.

Tom was hardly listening. He would just as soon leave his bag and get out of there. He wanted to disappear.

"Can one of these really save your life?" she asked playfully.

He stared stupidly at the mask in her hands.

"You know what I'll bet? I'll bet you look great in this thing."

She took another step closer and lifted the mask up over Tom's head, holding it there. He could feel her breath on his face.

"Tell me something, Tommy," she said quietly. Her grin morphed into something vaguely malicious. "When you were watching me last night on the dance floor, what were you thinking?"

"Last night?" he stammered. "I wasn't—"

"Were you surprised? Shocked to see me with another woman? Maybe it turned you on just a little bit?"

Tom's senses had hit overload. He didn't speak.

"You're telling people I'm gay. Maybe you're right. But I don't think I'm all the way there just yet."

"I didn't...I mean, I'm not..."

Loretta violently jerked the mask down over his head.

# Chapter 22

**D**ana Siegel sat in a darkened TV studio tearing into the sandwich he picked up at The Lord Byron—the DuPont Circle place where he had his name engraved on a barstool—on his way in for his late shift at CON-NET. Between bites he leaned into his viewfinder, training his lens on the two figures in Loretta's suite. The studio was meat-locker cold. He absently reached down to pull up his socks to ward against the chill, forgetting that he had stopped wearing socks.

His friends called him Bugsy. He was in semiretirement after a long run as an ABN cameraman. Never a skilled lens man—he had always been indifferent to the technical and artistic aspects of his work—the man had an uncanny knack for being in the right place at the right time with a camera on shoulder or a mic in his hands. Bugsy was a legend.

He came up at a time when the TV news industry was a realm of fantasy. Nobody expected the news divisions to actually make money. They were a bauble accruing to the intangible asset of prestige. Families tuned in every night, frozen fish sticks fried and plated, to be force fed every prosaic detail of world events. Anchors were deities, any talk of ratings apostasy. It was beneath the high-minded pursuit of journalistic enterprise and an inherent conflict of interest to worry about how many people actually watched your newscast. No one had ever heard of the term "audience demographic."

These days every ABN Wednesday-morning conference call with New York concluded with a grim recitation of the numbers, inevitably down in every metric. Yet in the face of substantial evidence that ABN News was heading for the cliff, managers spouted unsupportable predictions of renewal and return to glory. They were chasing unicorns to the edge of oblivion, and everyone was expected to come along into the abyss.

Each cameraman was now a one-man band, hauling light, camera, and sound gear all over town and expected to shoot a presser, an interview, and a stand-up in one day's work and still get off the clock before kicking into overtime. Every day was a ratings knife fight, and the network news was now run like any other business in America. Dana understood all that. But that didn't mean that he had to like it. The game had changed. The whole thing had gone stale. He might as well have been selling slacks at the local discount retailer.

It certainly hadn't started out this way. On the afternoon of his first day on the job Dana was in The Lord Byron, putting up with hazing by the veteran techs and trying to gain their respect by matching them beer for beer, when the phone behind the bar rang. It was for him, and when he put the receiver to his ear, he could hear chaos in the newsroom.

"Listen to me carefully, Bugsy." It was his assignment editor, panicked. "Grab all your gear and get your ass down to National right now. There's an ABN charter waiting for you. Get on it." *Well, OK,* thought Dana, *my own charter!* "And grab anyone else from our shop who is down there with you. Take them too."

"Will do, boss!" Dana cheerily replied. Just his first day on the job and he was already flying a charter to…where was he going?

"Dallas, for chrissakes!" cried the editor. "Don't you have your radio up? The president's been shot!"

Two days later he was in the garage of the federal building, waiting to film Lee Harvey Oswald's perp walk. A camera was up on his shoulder. His fellow rookie Johnny Stofko was on sound, tethered to Dana by audio cable. They had been there for hours.

There was a commotion down the hall, and moments later Oswald finally appeared, flanked by the cop wearing a cowboy hat. At that moment Dana felt someone rush by his elbow. It was the man in a fedora that he and Johnny had been chatting with most of the morning. The man had expressed some harsh opinions about Oswald, but so had everyone else in America that day.

That man was Jack Ruby. Dana pulled out from a tight shot just in time to record the images of him blowing Lee Harvey Oswald to hell. That was his first major journalism award.

Five years on, Vietnam, out on the town to celebrate the New Year. Shots come downrange. Dana turns to see a man's face splash in a gout of blood and brains. He runs for the American embassy carrying his camera and a few extra canisters of film. Ten minutes after he gets there the Vietcong heave over the walls.

Dana's shots of the carnage, of the desperate zeal of the commandos as they ran heedlessly into a curtain of death, were the definitive image of the Tet Offensive, making liars of generals, diplomats, and the president of the United States. The revolution was now televised. TV news had changed the world.

Twelve years later and Dana is standing outside the Hilton on Connecticut Avenue. President Reagan raises his hand to wave at well-wishers when a freak masquerading as a reporter opens fire. Dana again does the simple thing: he pulls to a wide shot and keeps a steady hand. Once again the world is shocked by something they see on Dana's footage.

He could have called it a life right there. Taken early retirement and played out the string in loafers and a five o'clock Old

Fashioned. He had seen more action in twenty years at ABN than most people see in three lifetimes. But he stayed on, and fortune smiled on him again when Minton Systems bought the network. His pile of profit-shared ABN stock became a much bigger pile of Minton stock.

When his old friend Johnny Stofko took a retirement buyout from ABN to join CON-NET, he started in on Dana to join him. They would still live the journalistic life of loose structure and new encounters and still be in proximity to Hill staff and in constant contact with some of the creamiest daddy's-girl talent the nation had to offer. No more hauling three hundred pounds of gear all over town to shoot stuff that might never make air. It was studio call-in shows, battalions of colorless eggheads in symposia, gavel-to-gavel coverage from the floor of each chamber. The place was a national treasure, impervious to ratings and dedicated to bringing the legislative process in all its stupefying boredom into American living rooms. Dana said what the hell and signed up.

The CON-NET operation was directly across an alley from Loretta Jean Polk's PAC office, and bearing unseen witness to her after-hours activity was turning out to be the principal benefit of the new gig for Dana. He developed an affection for her that went beyond the usual slobbering lust. Until now, he had remained reliably libidinous. This was the first time his carnal desires had ever been clouded by a paternal instinct, and it bothered him. It was late in the game for a mid-life crisis, but now he felt one coming on. He made panicky adjustments, adopting new habits designed to halt the spiral into a doddering old age. He affected a youthful élan by going sockless, wedging his bare, burled feet into a pair of Italian loafers. Now, as he absently reached to pull up a missing sock, he only scratched at a bald, bony ankle that betrayed his age to all the world. He was no bon vivant. He was but an old fool suffering the price of vanity.

For weeks he had spent his idle moments at work sitting alone in the dark and staring across the alley into Loretta's suite. Then one recent day he watched as she dialed a number she read off a slip off paper. Not three seconds later his cell phone rang.

"Hello, Dana!" It was Loretta. She was standing at the alley window, waving.

Ten minutes later they sat face-to-face on a bench under the barrel vault of Union Station. He half expected to be greeted by cops and arrested as a peeping tom, or at least to be faced with an indignant woman and a restraining order. Instead, Loretta had a proposition.

A bad man wouldn't leave her alone. She was wondering if Dana could protect her. If he could just do his usual thing from across the alleyway—and she wasn't in the least upset with him for watching her. Quite the contrary! She was flattered! But she was in trouble, and she needed to take out a little insurance against a certain individual who was trying to spread lies about her and do harm to her reputation. What this person really was interested in was blackmailing her for sex, she sadly explained, and by recording his unwanted advances on videotape, Dana would be helping by giving her all the evidence she would need to expose his plot.

"I hate it when guys get all freaky just because I happen to be a nice person. Some guys just get the wrong idea," she lamented.

"I might have known," Dana said to himself when he saw who was at her door. Salta. A pretty boy who gets by on razzle-dazzle. Lazy. The kind of guy who acted like the camera guys were there for the sole purpose of making him look like a movie star. Demanding crap like little can lights to make their corneas shine. "I'm a winter," Salta once informed Dana, as if that were supposed to mean a fucking thing. Now what he witnessed was breaking Dana's heart.

He watched in angry silence as he peered through his view-finder. The cable he had forgotten to disconnect from his camera snaked along the carpet, into a wall, above a drop ceiling, and down into the CON-NET control room, plugging into the mas-sive director's panel where Johnny Stofko sat dumbstruck. There was some kind of peep show coming from his friend Dana's camera output, and Johnny stared at the monitor with a mix of disbelief and a mounting thrill. In one especially intense moment his hand went slack, allowing the sandwich Dana had brought him from The Lord Byron to drop directly onto the array of but-tons on the switching board.

# CHAPTER 23

*"The relationship of a journalist to a politician should
be that of a dog to a lamppost."*

—H.L. Mencken

Tom woke up and confronted the brand new realities of his world.
The story that was going to make him famous was a set-up. His
finances were a wreck, the prognosis grim. His best friend was
betraying him. His professional and ethical standards lay in ruin,
demolished by Loretta Jean Polk.

Overall, he felt great.

Climbing into bed last night, he wondered whether he would
still respect himself in the morning. He did. He was actually kind
of proud. The endorphins issued from his glands into the atrium

of his heart, pumped through his capillaries, and back again. Any regrets were swept away in the wash.

How liberating it was to throw it all away in one impetuous moment! He hadn't understood how badly he'd needed to let go, to cede control of his destiny to a force of nature. It might have been better if the person who delivered him from his despair weren't an actual member of Congress. But that was a trifling point in the wave of his euphoria.

He was bounding out the door almost an hour ahead of schedule and got a seat on the Metro all to himself, a rare treat. He extended his legs out into the aisle and let his head fall back against the window. He resolved to contact Loretta Jean first thing once he was in the Capitol. When he got to his booth he was thrilled to find a manila envelope sitting on his chair with a handwritten note that read: "Tommy. Here's the *real* story." Then, "PS, it was wonderful spending time with you last night."

He leaned out and called to Gil. "Did you happen to see anybody come in this morning and drop something off in here?"

"Yeah. A page," Gil said, more crotchety than usual.

"Well, what did he look like?"

Gil picked up his computer mouse, rattled it violently for a moment, and slammed it back onto its pad. "He looked like every other page. A slack-jawed, pimply kid who apparently didn't own a comb. And his goddamn hair was purple." He glared at Tom. "Any other questions?"

"Right. No. Thanks."

Tom went back into his booth and opened the envelope to find an executive summary of an SEC report. It outlined a months-long investigation of Minton, including allegations of hiding losses through sham subsidiaries and other financial irregularities. In the margin there was a personal note: "I'm calling a subcommittee hearing for next week. Be there?"

"Thanks, Loretta Jean," Tom said to himself. She had sent him a gift better than flowers. It was a perfect coda to their encounter. Things were looking up.

Just then Billy burst in through the booth door. "Have you fucking seen this?" He was frantically pointing to the monitor.

"Don't you ever knock?"

BOP was on with the sound down. A grainy clip was playing on a loop. It looked like footage from a surveillance camera of some kind of sexual encounter. Billy was highly agitated.

"What a piece of shit your channel is." And to think this guy used to be his best buddy. "What is this?"

"This, my friend, is democracy in action."

Tom looked again and his heart stopped. The woman in the picture was impossible to make out. She was kneeling over the man. No, her knees were actually atop his chest. The man appeared to be naked, save for a large black bio mask over his head.

"Who are they?" Tom managed to ask.

"I have no idea. The guy is wearing a fucking gas mask, and she's goddamn Catwoman. Whoever she is, she's smokin'! Now *this* is news. Damn! Look at her working that guy over!"

Tom suddenly felt disconnected from himself, as if his nervous system had shut down in an involuntary reflex of self-preservation. It had to be Dickey. He had to be behind it somehow. He must have had Loretta under surveillance.

He had enough of his wits to understand that he mustn't let Billy see him panic. "When did BOP become a porno channel?"

"That's the beautiful part! It's a fucking legitimate news story!" Billy was beside himself with glee. "Check it out, because you won't believe this: last night the Senate was in late yakking about something. Ol' Bobby Dove is on the floor talking about the Peloponnesian War or some shit. The Spartans laid siege to this, the Athenians blockaded that, and how it all so resembles the modern day, what with all the parallels to the Middle East. It's just fucking killing me because I've got to hang around in my booth and watch the floor feed of this crap when I'm late for cocktails down the avenue. Bobby gets to the Pericles funeral oration, and he's really getting wound up, hands flying all around and his watch chain bouncing off his vest. It looks like he's fixin' to stroke out right there at his desk. All of a sudden, BOOM! We're off the Senate floor and onto Spanktravision. Somebody hits the wrong button someplace and presto, change-o! It's grab the lotion and tissue, boys!"

The loop rolled nonstop. The whole thing lasted maybe ten seconds before it started all over again.

"You mean this sleaze was seen by thousands of losers sitting home watching the Senate floor last night?" Tom said evenly.

"Can you believe it? It's like they decided to run a nasty clip from *Caligula* over another one of Bobby Dove's lectures on the classical world." The Bob Guccione epic was Billy's favorite movie ever. He claimed to have seen it eleven times.

"Yeah, but I mean, is this a porno tape, is this live, or what is this?" Tom looked for any hint of recognition.

"Not sure. We called the Senate Rules Committee. They're in charge of floor feeds. The chairman is about to put out a statement calling for a complete investigation."

"Yeah, but who are they?"

"What, you think we're keeping it a secret? If I had any idea who this chick was, I'd be staked out at her door myself. And I'd be damn sure to have on clean shirt and a part in my hair. This babe is a savage!"

Tom stared vacantly at the monitor as the clip played again.

"You still with me?" Billy waved an open palm in front of his face. "The story stopped running thirty seconds ago."

Tom's eyes came back into focus in time to see Billy on his way out of the booth. "I'll just close the door behind me," he laughed. "You look like you might need to relieve some stress."

This was a calamity. Tom had had his bio mask on, and at some point Loretta had put on her own black latex mask. But with MPEGs and JPEGs, broadbands and GIFs and the rest, it was only a matter of time before somebody recognized one or the other and pieced it together. And even if what aired on CON-NET lasted just those few seconds, someone somewhere probably had the raw tape of the whole encounter.

He picked up the receiver to dial Loretta's office just as the phone rang with the morning conference call from New York. He had half a mind to blow it off, but he shoved aside his panic and refocused.

Tom took a series of deliberate, deep breaths. This is what he had been building up to for weeks, his moment to drop the bomb. The new congressional investigation of Minton, revealed by the gift from Loretta that she had sent with the purple-haired page. If he were going to go down in a sex scandal, it would be in a blaze of glory.

Tom hated clichés. Everything happens for a reason…One door closes and another opens…It's always darkest before the dawn. Folk wisdom for simpletons, all of it, he believed. Opiates for the stupefied masses, ensuring their acceptance of inevitable defeat in a game that has always been rigged against them.

But what a perverse world! He had lost the story in a way that made no sense logically or metaphysically. Now he had a scoop every bit as big as the one he lost. It had taken an act of reckless surrender to strip him of his conceits, to rediscover his virtue. Now he was reborn. Sweet irony! His cynical ambition almost cost him whatever chance for happiness he may have had in life. Now here he was, a liberated man, giddy with optimism. And all because he had given himself over to fate. Let the chips fall where they may.

The conference call had begun. A disembodied voice in New York was presenting the usual glum recitation of the ratings. Tom could feel the darkness descending through his speakerphone from two hundred miles away. It was a litany of doom, delivered with all the morale-boosting brio of a funeral dirge. Total audience numbers were down, as they were in all key demographics. Even the oldsters were leaving.

A perfect day for a blockbuster story. He patiently waited his turn as the producers heard pitches from the big-city bureaus: Dallas, Chicago, Denver, New York. They all had bubkes. The call was going from depressing to desperate.

"Tom Salta, yer up. What's happening in the House of Reprehensibles?" Tom leaned in to the speakerphone and summoned his best This-Just-In Walter Winchellese.

"Good morning. ABN has learned that a key congressional panel has evidence of fraud and malfeasance at a major American corporation and is set to launch an investigation. The committee has subpoenaed company documents, taken what will turn out to be an explosive affidavit from a whistleblower, and hopes for hearings for next week." He leaned back, pausing for a moment to allow it all to sink in.

There was total silence. On any given morning there were fifty network producers and talent on the call. Tom envisioned every one of them at this moment grabbing for the edge of the conference table as they picked themselves up off the floor.

"Well, Tom, don't keep us in suspense. What is the name of the company?"

"That's the beauty part," Tom said.

"We're all ears."

"It's none other than the mighty Minton Systems Corporation." His normally dulcet tones had a tremulous quaver. He had forgotten to breathe.

"Minton," the senior repeated flatly.

"You heard it here first."

There was a long pause. Tom could hear whispering around the table.

The senior came back on the line. "How solid is your source on this?"

"Very solid. We have a source on the committee who has supplied us with the letter to Minton, as well as the affidavit." He used the more modest "we" knowing it was understood that he really meant "I."

"We also have copies of the subpoenas. We can use them for graphics."

Tom heard a phone ring in the conference room in New York. Then more unintelligible whispering.

The senior came back on the line. "Tom, do you think it can hold until tomorrow night?"

Tom was floored. What kind of message would spiking the story send to Loretta? He would be exposed as powerless in her eyes, lacking pull at his own network. What if she lost faith in him? "Well, I suppose it could. Although there is no guarantee that it won't show up on BOP tomorrow morning."

"I guess we're going to have to think this through together, Tom," the senior said in a tone that filled Tom with a sense of dread. "We were actually thinking that we'd like for you to have a look at this Senate tape thing and tell us if we can do the story in a way that isn't too sleazy."

He should have known as soon as he saw the video running on BOP that it would come to this. The fact that the tape appeared in connection with the US Senate was going to give everyone a plausible excuse to air what was essentially a second-rate soft-porn video. And he was the costar. Dread gave way to nausea. The irony had turned bitter. Tom may have finally found the limit of how far he would go to get on the air.

"I really have to say that I think it would be a mistake not to go with the Minton story tonight," he said. "I mean, aside from the fact that the exclusive may not hold, we're talking about something that could have a very significant impact on the American economy."

"Not to mention our 401(k)s," cracked a voice in the back of the room.

"We understand your concerns, Tom, we really do. But to be honest, the research shows a bit of scandal fatigue out there, at least as far as these accounting shenanigans go," he said. "And I'm hearing you say that at this point all we have is some paper. Subpoenas and what have you. That's a little dry, visually speaking. Too much process. Not enough pictures."

The rational man stays calm when confronted with absurdity. He laughs in the face of nonsensical hypocrisy. So now, as he giggled uncontrollably, Tom was heartened.

"It's your show," he said, laughing. "I'd just like to point out for the record that you have asked me to provide you with more scoops. This here is a drop-dead exclusive. That means that I've come through on my end. So please don't come back to me when it's on the front page of some website and tell me that I should have pushed you harder to do it tonight."

"I'll tell you what let's do," said the New York guy, back to being fed up with Tom. "Let's hold it over until tomorrow. That way we can brainstorm. Let the thing develop a little bit. Maybe find a small investor who would be affected by the congressional probe. Give it a little human touch. Take it out of DC."

Tom felt a deep belly laugh welling up and dove for the mute button. He composed himself and hit it again. "This has nothing to do with Minton being the corporate parent of the network, does it?" asked the rational man.

The ambient chatter at the other end of the line stopped.

"You're pushing it, Tom."

Tom kept his mouth shut.

"OK, fine," the senior sighed. "Let's all listen very closely. This program will always base our reporting on an objective sense of what is news and what isn't. The first question we have to ask ourselves is always, how does this story personally affect the life of the average viewer out there? The question is *not* what each or any of us have to win or lose if a particular story airs. That thought must never—*will* never—enter into the equation. Is that clear?"

It all sounded so perfunctory. "How does a secret video of anonymous lovers affect the life of the average viewer?" Tom asked.

"OK, Tom. I don't know what you think you can gain by being petulant, but if you think you're getting out of doing the Senate video story, you're wrong. We're doing that story, and you will report it. And I'd watch it with the wise mouth if I were you. You're on thin ice around here as it is."

"Fuck you," is what an irrational man would have replied. Tom suppressed another giggle. He said nothing.

# CHAPTER 24

Within minutes the clip went viral in a very big way. Tom was getting e-mails from people inhabiting every random corner of his life. His mother shared it on Facebook. All asked a different version of the same question: "Have you seen this shit?" All attached a link to the Loretta tape taken from what aired on CON-NET. Tom's hands were trembling each time he opened a new e-mail file, fearing that it would contain the raw, full-length video. True, he would still be wearing his biohazard hood and Loretta a Catwoman mask. They would still be hard to ID. But if either of them were revealed, the other's anonymity wouldn't last past lunchtime. He had wanted to be famous, but he didn't want to be Paris Hilton.

He stepped out of his booth, and it seemed the clip was playing everywhere. Colleagues and competitors called to one another, asking if they could fucking believe this shit and offering sarcastic critiques of the action on screen. Modern constraints against sexual innuendo in the workplace—never much in evidence in a gallery full of caustic, profane reporters to begin with—were completely dispensed with. It was a get out of jail free card for the unreconstructed lechers among them.

Even Gil was not immune. He sat struggling with his computer mouse, right clicking when he should have been left clicking, trying to play the clip. The fact that it filtered all the way down the electronic food chain to Gil erased all hope of getting out of having to do this story tonight. If Gil had his face in a computer screen, it was a bona fide cultural phenomenon. A young gallery staffer leaned over Gil and patiently explained the step-by-step process required to start Loretta's digitized motor. "Yes, go ahead. Click there. Right. No, I mean correct." He finally just decided to commandeer Gil's mouse and do it himself.

"Make it go again," Gil ordered the staffer when it was over. Tom watched him now, looking for a glimmer of recognition. Gil was the only person to have seen him in his bio mask.

After a second viewing he sat motionless, his hands joined under his chin as if here were down at the National Gallery contemplating a Rubens. His eyebrows furrowed. He raised his head and looked across the room. He had Tom in his sights.

Tom fled. He couldn't stand the thought of being shamed before Gil, a man he openly ridiculed but secretly esteemed.

He needed time to think. Statuary Hall called to him with the reassuring din of a thousand tourists and their murmuring echo. He entered the hall, but stayed in the shadows, walking behind each state's tribute in bronze and stone, finally settling against the onyx pedestal of King Kamehameha in a loincloth.

The bells calling members to the chamber rang out, heralding a series of votes. Tom figured it was as good a time as any to hunt down Loretta and give thanks for last night, as well as for the gift she had delivered to him this morning. He wondered if she knew about the video clip.

He walked around the cloakroom to the Speaker's Lobby, an anteroom just off the floor of the House chamber where baroque portraits of long-forgotten House speakers hung in a clutter along the walls, their mutton-chopped jowls immortalized in oil. The scene they kept watch over today was not much different from when they walked the same floor tiles, save for the paucity of modern members with facial hair. Congressmen still lounged in wingback chairs, smoking cigars or cigarettes and producing nimbus formations of carcinogens, oblivious to, or simply unconcerned with, the two very pregnant reporters who stood amid the haze trying to do their jobs. The space was a throwback to a more romantic era of backroom bosses and political machines. A total anachronism, almost subversive in its political incorrectness. Its existence in the modern age was a window to the true nature of the political animal: primordial in its tastes, protective of its turf, and open to reform only when publicly shamed. Every other federal building in town had long ago banned smoking, but this wasn't just another building. This was the home of the sovereign Congress, a coequal branch of government. The fact that other spaces were smoke-free provided a means to make a subtle point: members allowed themselves the pleasure of an indoor smoke for the simple reason that they could.

Reporters were forbidden on the House floor itself, so Tom filled in his name on an index card and handed it to a doorkeeper. "Can you pass this to Loretta for me?"

"I assume you're referring to Congresswoman Polk?" asked the doorkeeper, rolling his eyes. He didn't wait for an answer before turning on his heel.

Tom searched the floor through the lead glass of the chamber doors. He found her standing in the back row surrounded by the usual coterie of admirers. Each took their turn to grasp her by the elbow with one hand and pat her back with the other. She smiled easily until the doorkeeper pushed his way through and slipped her Tom's card. She glanced at it, quickly crumpling it into her palm.

Tom waited for twenty minutes. The round of votes was nearing an end, and she still hadn't made a move toward the Speaker's Lobby, and when she slipped her voting card in the reader for the last time she abruptly turned toward the rear of the chamber, bade good-bye to her groupies, and headed to the farthest exit.

Tom ran out of the lobby and around a corner in the hall outside in pursuit. He caught a glimpse of Loretta walking alone just before she disappeared behind a row of fluted columns. He kept running, alarming members and staff traumatized too many times by false threats and frantic evacuations. By the time he overtook her, she was on her way down the East Front steps, quickly yet gracefully navigating the granite atop four-inch heels.

"You didn't even give me a chance to thank you," Tom cooed from over her shoulder.

She turned with a pretend perkiness tinged with ferocity. "Thank me for what?"

Loretta kept walking, through clots of tourists and school groups along the plaza. Tom kept after her, and as she crossed Independence, he tried again. "Hey, can I please just talk to you for a minute?"

"Let me suggest that you contact my press secretary," she said, still smiling. "I don't do ambush interviews."

He couldn't believe that anyone, even a politician, could be so cold. He had been so buoyant with expectation all morning. He stayed with her, walking in silence all the way back to her Hill office, hoping that maybe when they were inside the building and afforded some kind of privacy she would drop the front of hostility.

Members of Congress are above suspicion on Capitol Hill, not required to subject themselves to the humiliation of walking through metal detectors like regular people. Everyone else had to go through security; the only exception was if you were in the company of a member. Then you could cruise right past the machines and the police detail that manned them. Another accommodation made to politicians too important to be inconvenienced with the strictures placed on the rest of the citizenry in the age of terror. The cops at the Cannon building door barely looked at Tom as they heartily greeted the congresswoman from Wyoming.

"He's not with me, fellas," Loretta said, jerking her thumb in Tom's direction. She kept walking as Tom circled back and through the magnetometer. By the time he made it through she was almost out of sight.

"Loretta Jean, wait!" Tom shouted down the marbled hall. He heard the old oak door of her office slowly creak on its hinges then release at the last and bang shut.

He ran to the door and threw it open. A young receptionist at the front desk looked up, startled, and for a split second they stared at one another until she saw something in Tom's eyes that told her that this guy was potentially deranged—perhaps a cyber stalker of Loretta's who had been blocked from her Twitter feed. It had happened before. Her hand reached for the phone.

That was Tom's cue to surrender all cerebral functions and shift to a cognitive plane where the primal imperative was dominant and reason ignored. He started for her private office. A young man reached out to stop him, and then another hand found Tom's shoulder. Tom paid them no mind, only pressing forward, opening the door to the inner sanctum and bursting inside.

She sat on a government-issue Naugahyde club chair, pretty as you please, betraying no panic, no alarm, as if people with their hearts on fire were running through her door on a regular basis. It was a continuation of the performance she had given on the House steps minutes ago, the chamber floor before that, and back through time to the moment she first met her now-dead husband.

Her plan had been to humiliate Salta: to thoroughly compromise him and to get it on video. It was her insurance policy, a copy of which she would send to Dickey and Stu, the equivalent of a dead fish wrapped in newspaper and delivered to their doorstep. She neglected to share that part of the plot with Dana, the cameraman. She realized now that was a miscalculation. The CON-NET clip was *not* part of the plan. Fortunately, she had taken steps to disguise her identity, narrowly averting a disaster that would have ruined everything. She didn't show it, but she was scared.

Now with Salta at her door she calmly reassured the staffers who had rushed to protect their boss, thanked them for their concern, and asked them to please close the door behind them on the way out.

"I just wanted to say hello and tell you how much I enjoyed spending some time with you last night," Tom ventured, lamely.

"Let me make myself perfectly clear," Loretta began. "I don't want to hear from you. I don't want you anywhere near me. I don't want to see your fool face. Ever," she said evenly. "Do you understand?"

"But I work here," Tom said dumbly, as if he could change her mind by challenging her premise. "And you might see my face on the news. I can't help that."

"You are a clown and a simpleton. It won't be long before you're doing sports somewhere in North Dakota."

"But what about the documents you left for me this morning?" he stammered.

"I left you nothing, you goddamned idiot," she said fiercely. "Now pretend like you have just a little self-respect and get out of my office."

# CHAPTER 25

*Well now I don't read that daily news, 'Cause it ain't
hard to figure where people get the blues.
They can't dig what they can't use,
If they stick to themselves they'd be much less abused.*

—"I Know a Little," Lynyrd Skynyrd

This time it was Gil who came into Tom's booth, closing the door behind him.

"You really are a goddamned idiot," Gil began.

"That seems to be the consensus." Tom didn't have the energy to argue or to wonder why Gil was making a personal appearance in his booth for the first time.

Gil was inscrutable, as always. "Don't complain, never explain," was his guiding motto. He was the son of an Iowa grain-elevator operator and a bank teller, who taught him that modesty is to be valued and the nail that sticks out gets hammered down. Flamboyance was his lifelong enemy. He had all the élan of Sergeant Joe Friday, unadorned in both appearance and personality.

He hated the phoniness and pandering that attended so much of what was considered essential for success in his beloved profession of broadcast journalism. It was no longer enough to report the news every evening as a chronological accounting of the day's events and the contextual facts surrounding them. It was to the point where the bedrock ideal of objectivity was looked on as a relic—like Tang from the Space Age—or even disparaged. Instead, everyone from the anchors to the weatherman was required to let us in on the "truth" and to reveal what was a "lie." No in-betweens. Nobody could ever be misguided, misinformed, or simply mistaken. You were either with us or against us, and you had better make up your mind in a hurry, because if you tried to perpetuate the canard of objectivity, then you were obviously a tool of the prevaricators and the enemy of all that was right and true.

Gil tried not to dwell on his anger. News was his religion and objectivity its gospel. He believed there was bound to be a reckoning soon.

"I know that it's you in that video," he told Tom.

Tom stared dumbly.

"And that your friend—if that's the correct word—is Congresswoman Polk," Gil continued, expressionless.

Tom paused to allow the first surge of adrenaline to wash through before asking, "How?"

"With a little help from the gallery staff, I was able to enhance the clip of you two and zoom in to confirm that the woman you were with has a tattoo on her ankle. Representative Polk has an identical tattoo."

Again, Tom had to pause for a moment to digest this information.

"I have attended several press conferences that featured a presentation from Ms. Polk," Gil explained. "On many of these occasions I have been compelled to kneel before the microphone stand in order to hear what is being said. As you know, I have become somewhat hard of hearing," he allowed, embarrassed to insert a personal element into his reporting. "At any rate, during my time at her feet, as it were, I have noted a small tattoo on the outside of Polk's left ankle. It is in the likeness of a butterfly. A monarch, I believe. The woman in the video has an identical marking." Gil stopped for a moment to let this sink in, then asked: "Do you dispute my assertion?"

"I stipulate to the facts as you have presented them," said Tom, mindlessly aping Gil's locution. Tom had often seen Gil literally at the feet of the powerful, wearing a pair of headphones and sweeping his Sennheiser microphone from speaker to speaker. After years in that position and with his eye for detail, he could probably list the shoe sizes of half the members of Congress.

Gil eyed Tom as a doctor would a patient who has just received a grim prognosis. "I am prepared to make you a deal. I will sit on the information that I have just related to you for two days. During that time, I want you to get on your horse and break whatever story has brought these frequent visits to the gallery by the majority leader's assistant, as well as your unfortunate encounter last night in Polk's suite."

Tom was confused. "But why—"

"Just get the story, Tom," Gil said brusquely. "I know what you're going to ask me, but the fact is that you obviously have a big head start. I could jump in and start from scratch, but there's no guarantee that I'll get anywhere. You're on to something big, that's obvious. But you had better hurry. I think you will agree that if a guy like me can manage to navigate my way clear to uncover the truth about who is in the video, then forget it. You're going to be found out and it's going to be huge news. And when that happens, you're a goner. So get to work."

That answered only part of Tom's question. "But what about this story, today. The one where you know the identities of the people being intimate on congressional TV?"

"Again, you have two days. Do whatever you have to do. If you don't break something big, then I will tell the world that it was you and Polk in the video," Gil said.

"I never wanted this to happen," Tom said, shaking. "I didn't think she—"

Gil waved him off with both hands. "I'm not hearing confessions today."

Tom tried to compose himself. "Don't you want to know what you're passing up?"

"As a matter of fact, I do not," Gil asserted. "Though something tells me it will be huge."

This did not compute for Tom. "Then why are you offering to sit on the video story?"

"Two reasons. First, it won't make a bit of difference in anyone's life, so why waste two minutes of a twenty-two minute program? I don't mean any offense to your physical attributes, but it's not worthy of that kind of attention."

Tom was filled with gratitude. Still, some part of him wondered how Gil's reasoning counted for anything. "What about the ratings?"

"I've come too far and lived too long to whore myself out. I don't want to be a part of it. All the bullshit out there will never be able to match solid, frontline reporting. There will always be a market for that. The garbage will shake itself out. All we need to do is stick to our knitting."

Tom was humbled. "I understand now," he said. "But what is the second reason?"

"Simple. I'm trying to motivate you because I like you. You make me laugh."

# Chapter 26

*Pride goeth before a fall.*

*—Proverbs 16:18*

The smirk Tom used as an all-purpose tool had been slapped right off his face. Gil had given him two days to finally get the story nailed down. His back was up against the wall, and he didn't give a damn what he had to do in order to save himself. All this bullshit started with Dickey and Stu, and so that's where he would begin.

"Have you ever been up inside the rotunda?" was Stu's quixotic response to Tom when he called demanding answers once and for all to the riddle of Loretta. A few minutes later Tom found himself watching Stu fumble with a ring full of keys, trying three before slipping the right one into the lock and opening the door to the base of a winding staircase.

The Capitol Dome is actually two domes, one set inside the other like Russian nesting dolls. A staircase runs between the two cast-iron eggs, corkscrewing its way to the top. There was a time when anyone could walk up on their own and have a look from the balustrade ringing the top of the inner dome down the 187 feet to the tourists below, as they in turn stared back up at the Brumidi fresco on the ceiling of the outer dome. Tom's grandfather told the story of how, as a kid growing up in an Italian ghetto where a Senate office building now stood, he and his barefoot friends would walk over to the Capitol and post themselves at the bottom to afford a better view up ladies' skirts.

Today you had to be escorted by someone in a position of influence if you wanted to make the climb. On any other day he would have been delighted for the chance to indulge mystical notions of his long-dead grandfather's presence in the trusswork. But not today. Today all this was an irritation and a potentially huge waste of time. Gil's clock was ticking.

On the phone minutes earlier, Tom had hit Stu with bellicose threats to reveal Dickey's original sordid proposition, alternated with abject pleas for help. "Let's just take this walk, and I promise that you won't be disappointed," was Stu's serene reply.

"The woman you saw with Loretta at that bar the other night is named Cornelia Livingwell," Stu began as they took the first step up. "Have you ever heard of her?"

The name rang a bell, but Tom was not in a mood to reflect.

"Cornelia Livingwell is a Minton lobbyist, which is interesting in and of itself, as I'm sure you will agree," Stu said.

"That's funny. I heard you were marrying a Minton lobbyist," Tom said obtusely.

Stu gave him a backward glance and continued. "What's even more interesting is that she also happens to be Zach Dickey's daughter."

They climbed on, the sound of grit on the bottom of their shoes sliding in synch onto each successive step, rhythmically, like a metronome.

The beat had a hypnotic effect on Stu. He spoke in time with the cadence. "Cornelia is in love with Loretta."

The implications were almost too much to process all at once. Tom took a moment to mentally rewind. "And that was her in the dance club?"

"Indeed it was."

Tom willed himself to keep moving. "I suppose that's why Dickey is trying to destroy Loretta," he said.

"Well, yes. Now he is. But that's Plan B."

Tom decided to just keep climbing and let Stu talk.

"Zach Dickey has known of their affair. And yes, he was against it. He was willing, and remains willing, to do everything he can do to stop it," Stu said.

"He hasn't given up?"

"Indeed not. But unfortunately for Zach, he has discovered that even though he can exert his will over almost everyone in this town and half of Tennessee, his power did not extend to the personal affairs of his own daughter. She told him not only that she loved Loretta, but that she hated him, her father, for putting his own career above her happiness."

Tom resolved to concentrate on only those facts necessary to get on the air with this story. "What was his reaction to that?"

"He came up with a solution that involved something he does control. Me."

"I don't follow you."

"Zach proposed a deal to his daughter. He would arrange for her to take a husband who would in turn agree to stand by and allow her to pursue any lifestyle she chose, so long as it wasn't done publicly so it would damage him with the base."

"That was Plan A, I assume."

"Plan A," Stu confirmed.

"I'm sorry, but I just have to hear this again," Tom couldn't help himself. "Am I to understand that Dickey was asking you to marry his daughter, knowing full well that his daughter was carrying on with another woman and had no interest in you?"

Stu kept climbing, silent. Tom cursed his inability to keep his mouth shut when another man was spilling his guts.

Finally Stu said, "All I ever wanted to be was a wonk." He sounded lost.

Tom tried to recapture the vibe. "So Dickey tried to force you to marry his daughter? Wow!"

Too late. "I came to this town twenty-five years ago as an idealist who wanted to be part of something that mattered," said Stu, launching on a tangent. "I was a conservative when we were in the wilderness, and the thought of us running this place and running the country was a joke. But I thought there was a way out. Washington was running on empty clichés that were trapping people in a cycle of dependency. The values of Washington were divorced from the real America. Reward for hard work or building a better mousetrap. Freedom to create, innovate, and prosper, instead of micromanaging lives. America wasn't American anymore. That's what I came here believing, and to this day I still do. There are a million things you can think about that make it all much more complicated, and for a while I questioned my convictions. But in the end I realized that those kinds of equivocations can only paralyze you."

*Come back to me now, Stu,* Tom thought. "So you resisted the idea? Of marriage, I mean."

"I came to this place with Zach Dickey," Stu continued, his voice disembodied, as if he were conversing with the stones. "I knew from the first time I met him that here was a man who shared my beliefs. And he wasn't just an idealist—the type that would spend years tilting at windmills. He understood the game of politics and he had a plan. The man had the mark of greatness. I could see that right away. It was a dream job with a dream boss."

They both stopped and squeezed over to the side to make room for a congressman and his guests who were descending from the summit.

"I've been with him all the way to the top," Stu said as they continued their march, "and for the most part I can say it's been a privilege. Until the last year."

Stu stopped. The two men looked directly into each other's eyes. "You've always seemed like a good soldier," Tom offered.

Stu motioned for him to resume the climb. "But not good enough. At least not for him."

"So what happened?"

"He offered me a half-million-dollar job at one of his connected K Street outfits if I would play this role of husband. Hell, the way he saw it, I was practically already a son, or at least a family member." There was an empathizing sadness in Stu's voice. "Making me his son-in-law was more like a demotion in his eyes."

"What about in *your* eyes?"

"Zach has lost his way. I had known that somewhere deep in my soul, but now all this. It's undeniable. I love the man, and in a way I love Cornelia. We've practically been brother and sister for years, and together we've cleaned up a lot of messes. A lot. But it's not about the cause anymore. This is about his megalomania. Out-of-control narcissism. Forget about my feelings and what I want. The fact that he thinks that his own daughter should live her life masquerading as something that she isn't is ridiculous. And shameful. It's the opposite of what he—what we—used to be about."

"All for the sake of appearances," Tom said.

"That's the sickest thing. He's convinced the holy rollers won't back him if his daughter marries a woman. I tried to explain to him that it's been done. He says that's different. That he's running at the top of the ticket, not as a last-minute choice for running mate. The values crowd can look the other way if the veep's daughter is a pervert, even though they still wonder why she wasn't dragged kicking and screaming to conversion therapy. But the nominee himself can't have offspring that have strayed onto the road less traveled. That's a divine message writ on stone to the base that tells them the Dickey family has fallen out of favor with God. And living among the damned is definitely not a characteristic they're looking for in a leader."

"I don't doubt it for a second," Tom said, not meaning that Dickey was cursed, but agreeing that's how the base would see it.

"You're a member of the godless media, so I expect you to laugh."

"Go on," said Tom. He would have admitted to being a werewolf if it meant Stu would keep talking.

"Cornelia is a sweet, intelligent woman. Unlike her father, there isn't a deceitful bone in her body. What you see is what you get. It just so happens that she prefers the company of women, or at least this one woman, and she can't change that even if she wanted to. She is who she is. She feels what she feels."

"But you guys are always pandering to them. Isn't this just a logical extension of what goes on around here all the time?"

"The last thing I did before coming over here was meet with the Values Caucus people. They want to withhold funding from the Smithsonian until they agree to construct an Adam and Eve diorama at the Museum of Natural History."

*Now there's a little item that I could turn around into a quick blog post for the website,* Tom thought.

"I can go along with stuff like that. No one gets hurt, and it's for the greater, long-term good of the cause. It motivates the wing nuts, and their support is what keeps us in the majority," Stu said. "But this thing with Cornelia is different. This is human sacrifice. It's grotesque."

"So you refused." Tom meant it not as a question but as a statement.

For the next several steps Stu said nothing. "Actually, no," he said in a whisper.

"Oh, Stu."

"I'm the classic stooge, aren't I?" he whimpered. "In the end I simply cannot say no to the man. I start out with bold intentions.

Of drawing a line in the sand. But when push comes to shove I simply bend to his will. This time is no different."

Tom dared not agree. At least not out loud.

"I went out and got a ring, then drove straight to her house with a bouquet of roses, ready to do my duty to the king. Of course, I knew that she had already basically told her father to go take a flying leap and that she would never agree to it. But I thought that somehow I could just drop by and make a goof out of it, use a little of that ol' Stu charm on her, and she would come around," he said with self-ridicule.

"Don't see how you could go wrong with that approach," Tom joked.

"So she opens the door, and I promptly fall to my knees and pop the question. I'm not much with romance, but I made a go of it. I went for the pity angle."

Tom tried to conjure the absurd scene.

"I mean, after all, nobody said it would have to last forever. And it wasn't like I was thinking that we would actually live and lie together as man and wife." Stu was rambling now, as if alone in the shower. "It requires a very limited emotional investment on her part. The only time she would have actually had to kiss me would have been at the altar, and even then she could have gotten away with a closed-mouth peck on the lips."

It didn't sound all that unreasonable. "So did you tell her all that?"

"I was on my knees on her front stoop," Stu was becoming emotional, "and I didn't want to ruin the moment by bargaining. As it happens, I did have a chance to reason with her, but only after I came to on her couch."

"You fainted?" Tom asked, incredulous.

"Not exactly."

"Don't tell me she knocked you out!"

"Technically, it was the door that she slammed that hit me in the head as I was doubled over after she kicked me in the genitals that knocked me out. It wasn't like she actually punched me in the nose."

"Ouch!" Tom said. Stu was trying to play it off, but he was clearly traumatized.

"I have tried to do my best," Stu said as tears stood in his eyes. "In the end it turns out not to be good enough, neither for Zach nor his daughter."

At that moment they reached the top of the stairs. Stu quietly walked over to the balustrade that ran around the ocular opening at the peak of the inner dome.

"They say that if you were to take the Statue of Liberty off her pedestal and set her down in the rotunda, the flames from her torch would just fit under the ceiling," Stu said wistfully. He was leaning over the side and looking straight down.

In high school, Tom and his friends would pile into a car after August two-a-day football practice and ride out to a flooded quarry in Dickerson. Boys with balls to spare but without the brains to match would prove their courage with epic leaps into the green water. It was their Acapulco. Each jump had a name—"Beetle," "Fourteen," and "Suicide" in order of ascension—and, factoring in the number of hippie chicks ringing the quarry walls, multiplied by the number of beers Tom had on the drive out, he was usually game for a jump. He never really thought twice about the height. These days, driving over the Bay Bridge brought on panic. And at this moment, without the benefit of booze to buck him up, and the fact that the surface far below wasn't a fathomless quarry but quarried granite, Tom was petrified.

They stared down at the ant-sized tourists. "I could tell you things about what goes on around here that would really make your scrotum shrivel," Stu said.

"Too late."

Stu shot him a look of disdain. "See, that's the problem with the media."

"Huh?" Tom was lost again.

"What you guys report, what people hear on the news? It's all about conflict and scandal. But when it comes to substance, what people get is like the perspective from up here," Stu said, looking down at tourists milling like amoeba in a microscope. "You guys need to spend more time getting into the nitty gritty of legislation, instead of giving everyone the view from 187 feet then moving on to the latest car chase."

It hardly seemed the time or the place for yet another disquisition on the failures of the mainstream media. Yet Tom continued to indulge Stu, who was acting wistful and strange and offbeat. That was a hopeful sign of more dirt to come.

"They call that 'process.' It's best for your career if you stay away from it. Seems the masses get bored," Tom said.

"But people need to know what is going on here *while* it's going on! You guys all want to wait until it's over before you report on stuff that is really important, stuff that affects people's lives." A nebulized spray of Stu's spit filled the space between them. "But by that time it's too late! How is the public supposed to have any kind of input into making laws?"

"Can we decree a fatwa on the media later? I'm in a bit of a rush," Tom said.

"I'm just looking for some clarification."

"Well, then let me say to you what I say to those self-important assholes on social media: change the goddamned channel if you don't like it. Sanctimony comes cheap."

Stu ignored him. "See those tourists down there soaked in the majesty of this place? They've spent their time and money to come from all over the country to see this. Look at them," Stu made a sweeping motion of his arm. "They're in awe of the history and the men who made it. Are you trying to tell me that they don't care about what happens here? Yet in your arrogance you have decided that they shouldn't be bothered with news of their own leaders."

"I challenge you to go down there and say the name 'Zach Dickey' to ten tourists," Tom replied. "The name might ring a bell for two of them, one of whom would identify him as an astronaut and the other as a celebrity transsexual."

"Exactly! You have proven my point," said Stu. "They don't know because you guys have decided that they don't want to know."

"They don't care about Washington. The ratings don't lie."

Stu visibly deflated. "The ratings. The polls," he said bitterly. "Name recognition and, God help us, branding. We're not a legislature anymore, we're a marketing firm. I'm so sick of it. Why are we here in the first place? It all seems so mendacious when we have the power to do something to empower people. To make their lives better."

Most people Stu's age, when they get depressed, they drink or listen to Dan Fogelberg albums, take a moment to wallow in self-pity. Not Stu.

Tom said, "Look, you can't force people to eat their broccoli just because you and I say it's good for them. And maybe if politicians stop acting like assholes willing to say anything or kiss anyone's ass for money, people would actually have more respect." Tom paused, then asked, "What is news?"

"News is what's important."

"Wrong. News, my friend, is the unexpected. Fifty percent of what happens here is expected and therefore isn't news. Another 45 percent is sophistry, polemics, and hot air. But I'll tell you what *is* news: corrupt elected national officials using their offices for personal gain. *That's* news."

Stu was lying on his chest atop the balustrade, his head hanging limp over the side.

"Look on the bright side," Tom continued. "Your beloved fat-turd tourists down there still think that their Congress is populated by men and women of honor. Corruption is still not considered a normative operating condition. See what I'm saying? It's unexpected. Therefore, it's still news."

"Has it occurred to you that your contempt for these tourists is an extension of your disdain for your audience?" Stu asked.

"Hadn't thought about it."

Stu fell into a long pause before another thought came to him. "You know what's depressing?"

Tom wondered what could be more depressing than being around Stu.

"Really soon, none of it's going to matter anymore. Anyone can find out anything at any time and in any way they want to find it. Congress will be a side show," Stu declared, raising himself back upright.

"That ship has sailed. Hate to break it to you."

Stu's face was blood filled and blotchy. "In any event, there's nothing left for me. I have been humiliated beyond even my tolerance for humiliation. I'm past salvation."

"Believe me, I know how you feel," said Tom.

A slight smile came to Stu. "You do and you don't."

"What do you mean?"

"You've been humiliated enough to make any other man run and hide. Yet here you are, still striving. You don't have the sense to realize you've been disgraced. Or maybe you don't have the decency to just go away and spare people the discomfort of being around you. Shame? Pride? Mere equivocations in the face of your colossal ambition. You're not unlike Zach Dickey himself."

Tom wasn't sure where this was going. "Um, you're talking about that thing the other day in the copy room, right?"

"Oh, come on," Stu said. "You're so good at playing the hardened cynic. But this isn't a game of beanbag. Honestly, what did you think was going to happen in Loretta's suite last night? "

Now it was Tom's turn to stare blankly down at the tourists.

"OK. Let me spell it out for you, because you really do need to know. It would be downright cruel to keep you in the dark," Stu said. "Dickey has the tape."

"I'm sure I don't know what you're talking about," Tom said.

"The tape that made it onto Senate TV last night."

"So does just about any staffer with a smart phone," Tom said. "They're all looking at it now."

"You're missing the point, sir. He knows it was *you*. For that matter, he knows it was you *and* Loretta. And he doesn't simply have the few seconds that aired on the Senate TV feed that is at this moment costing the American economy millions in lost productivity. He's got the raw tape. No pun intended," Stu said. "I believe this sort of thing is referred to as 'the director's cut.'"

Stu was wrong. Tom could feel shame. He felt it last night when Loretta destroyed his bogus case against her. He felt it now at this minute. And he felt stupidity, for imagining a veil of secrecy saturated by a million Internet hits would hold strong.

"Let me give you a lesson in how power is gained and kept in Washington," Stu said. "When Dickey was in Vietnam flying helicopters, he befriended a cameraman for one of the news networks covering the war. I believe you may know this fellow? My understanding is that, until recently, he was a colleague of yours at ABN."

"Bugsy," Tom said quietly.

"Yes, yes, that's it. The man's name is actually Dana, but for reasons that are unclear to me, his friends call him 'Bugsy.' Stu was warming to the role of Professor Higgins. "At any rate, it seems that Dickey got a call this morning from this Bugsy chap.

Quite upset, he was, clearly. He proclaimed rather loudly—I could actually hear him through the receiver as he spoke with Leader Dickey—that Loretta was nothing but a cheap such and such who had betrayed his trust and used him as a pawn in some unspeakably lascivious plot. Impugned dear Congresswoman Polk's character in frightfully coarse terms, I must say. Apparently, he doesn't think much of you either."

"Yes. I'm aware of that."

"He and Dickey have remained thick as thieves. He's a useful cog in the machine. You didn't know?" Stu taunted. "Anyway, it turns out this Bugsy can be added to the long list of those to have fallen under Loretta's spell, seeing as how she somehow arranged to have him surreptitiously film your encounter. But this time she may have gone too far, since what he saw was not what he expected to see. Left him quite enraged, actually. He sent the tape over this morning to Dickey. He's got it in his possession right now."

"I'm fucked."

"Quite so."

Tom looked once more over the marble railing and wondered if Stu was right, that the only decent thing would be to remove himself from society. All it would take would be for him to simply stand up on the railing and jump. The granite would take care of the rest. To his knowledge, a rotunda suicide had never been done. First in the nation. He'd get wall-to-wall coverage and go out in a blaze of TV glory.

"I want you to have this," Stu said, handing Tom a manila folder. "I can't let him continue to destroy people's lives."

"No more documents! How are these any different from what you left in my booth this morning?"

"I didn't leave anything in your booth."

"An SEC investigation? Of Minton? Malfeasance? It wasn't Loretta. I'm clear on that." It took several seconds of Stu mutely grinning for Tom to realize that he had been had. Again. "None of this rings a bell, does it?"

Stu sighed. "Zach is out of control. I have no idea what he is up to now. But I think it's safe to say that he sent you another bum tip out of sheer desperation. He knew about you and Loretta in her suite. He exploited that information by pretending to be her. Clever man. But he's gone off the rails. It's a tragedy."

Tom wondered how many people on the other end of the morning call dumped their Minton stock. "I don't know why I should even bother to look at this stuff. The last batch was nothing but a pile of garbage."

"What I have given you will mean the end of Dickey and the end of me. This is the only answer. This charade has got to stop."

"What do these actually prove?"

"I have taken the liberty of writing a script for you," Stu said. "I think it spells it all out very clearly."

Tom laughed out loud. "A script? You mean for the news? Is that ethical?"

"Spare me," Stu said. "It's obvious by now that instead of your brain, you think with parts of your anatomy not designed for that purpose. Like your testicles, for example."

Tom couldn't argue with that.

"You'll find the goods are all there to back it up," Stu said.

Little color-coded tabs were affixed to the pages, with a handy index on the top sheet to guide him along. There were footnotes and an appendix with cross-references, and a glossary of technical terms. There was an executive summary. Finally, there was a thumb drive in a small envelope that had been taped to the inside cover of the folder.

"They're getting married," Stu said.

Tom looked up from the documents. "I thought you said she kicked you in the balls. Or was that her way of saying 'I do'?"

"I didn't say *we*. I said *they*."

"I think I lost the thread. Who's 'they'?"

"Cornelia and Loretta. They're getting married this weekend. Saturday. They're in love."

Tom had to steady himself at the railing. He dumbly looked at the folder in his hand. Altogether it was going to be a hell of a story.

"You like?" Stu seated on the balustrade. He smiled serenely.

"I don't know what to say."

"Don't let me down, Tom," Stu said. And with that he leaned back over the railing and let go.

# Chapter 27

Even from where Tom stood, halfway down the block from Cornelia Livingwell's house in Glover Park, he could hear the keening.

It was over now. There really was no reason for Tom to even be there. His script had been written and approved by half the news division, from the standards and practices people straight up to the president and beyond, to the CEO of Minton. He had laid down his voice track, and at this very moment audio was being married up to video back in the bureau. Every minute or so Tom compulsively reached for his phone and checked the battery life—reassurance in case he was called in for a last-minute tweak. The story was due to air at the top of the evening news: 6:30 p.m.

Cornelia had been sobbing since the moment "Breaking News" first flashed on the cables hours ago announcing the spectacular and gruesome suicide of a top aide to Majority Leader Zach Dickey. Coverage was still wall-to-wall.

Earlier that day Tom had stood on her doorstep with his heart in his throat. "Door knocks" were part of a local reporter's job, a part he hated. Intruding on a family that had just lost a loved one to a drug deal gone bad, or a husband whose wife had just driven into the lake with the kids strapped in the backseat. On-camera hysterics were the goal. Ratings gold. He always wanted to tell them that they didn't have to talk to him. But he didn't and, weirdly, they did.

This was different. This was his story. So he dutifully presented himself on Cornelia's stoop. In a concession to conscience and decency, he instructed the camera crew to stay in the SUV idling at the curb and not jump all up in her face. He wore a wireless mic.

When the door cracked open, he tensed, expecting fury. But her eyes were hollow, her cheeks streaked black with mascara.

"Come in," she said.

They sat facing each other in her front room, and he told her of Stu's last grasp at redemption before letting go. That Stu had spilled everything: the conspiracy, the skullduggery, and the espionage. Her romance with Loretta Jean and their plans to marry. That she would be a central part of the story to air in the morning. He asked if she had anything she wanted to say, any questions.

She only had one. "Where is your camera crew?"

"They're in the truck outside. I didn't want to intrude."

"What a strange thing to say," Cornelia replied. "Bring them in. I want this on the record."

A rambling thirty minutes and three cigarettes later, Tom had firsthand confirmation—on camera, from Cornelia—of everything that Stu had given him.

# CHAPTER 28

**D**ickey's protective detail sat at the curb in a big black Tahoe. The boss had made it clear to them: if Tom Salta showed his face within a hundred yards of his daughter, call. If Salta left before Dickey could get there, follow him. If he parked, puncture his goddamn tires. Do whatever you needed to do to make sure Dickey knew where to find him.

Inside the house, Cornelia recounted every detail. She let go of any inhibition or reluctance; she paused only to light up, never to wipe her eyes or soothe her thirst. She wasn't angry, at least not visibly. She was disconsolate, half-dead, in shock. She spoke as if Tom weren't even there. It was a catharsis by confession. She only raised her exhausted eyes to him when she came to the end, asking if there were anything else he needed to know so that the story would be sure to ruin her father.

Tom didn't know if it was the ethical thing to do. He didn't pause to think about abstracts like objectivity or detachment or what standards and practices might say. He had a visceral need to hug her. Because she was in pain. Because her world had exploded the moment Stu's head hit the floor of the rotunda with a sickening pop. Because in the presence of real courage he saw that he was and always had been a coward.

So he embraced her. He bent to put his arms around her even as she sat, limp and wordless, her chin resting on his shoulder.

That was how Dickey found them when he burst through the front door at a run, snarling, "You're a fucking dead man."

The thumping of her father's boots on the hardwood floor shook Cornelia from her trance. She screamed as he lunged for Tom, fingers rigid, guided missiles targeted for the throat. Tom juked to his left and made a break for the door.

"Roll tape! Roll tape!" Tom shouted to his crew.

He made it as far as the threshold and onto the porch before one of Dickey's boots caught him squarely on the right buttock, sending him sprawling onto the lawn. As he fell, Tom calculated the best case scenario: the beating to come would leave marks dramatic enough to be noticed on camera, but not lasting scars. Flat on his back, he saw his camera crew outside of the house, rolling as they ran for the truck. It would be one hell of a piece of video.

Dickey's cops were under the mistaken impression that pounding the crap out of someone on camera—especially a lowlife reporter—would look bad for Dickey. It took all three of them to hold him back. The last thing Tom and his crew saw as they sped away was Dickey in a murderous rage, throwing punches at the people sworn to protect him.

# CHAPTER 29

The moments after Stu's suicide were a blur. At first Tom thought it was a gag, a punch line to button up Stu's too-good-to-be-true tale of love and betrayal. He rushed to the balustrade expecting to see Stu squatting on a cornice, looking up at the terrorized Tom and laughing at him for being a sucker. "Dickey's own daughter in love with Loretta? Dickey talking me into proposing to Cornelia to save him from political ruin? Me killing myself because she wouldn't have me? To redeem my honor?"

Inconceivable.

But those things did happen. Tom already knew he would live with the vision for the rest of his life. Understanding *why* it all happened would take time.

Stu could have just quit, just walked away from the humiliation and anguish. So he was disillusioned. That's life! Was it worth willfully falling to a public death because of your high-minded ideals? People come to Washington to do good and end up doing well. Why didn't Stu get the joke?

Of all the reporters in Washington, Stu had climbed those stairs with Tom. He'd prepared the dossier for him. He'd looked straight at him when he let go. Tom had been entrusted with something—he wasn't sure how to define it, but he sensed it was important. Sacred. He wasn't about to let the mob get a hold of it and turn it into a cartoon.

So he ran for it. He took the spiraling steps two at a time back down between the domes, his right hand cupped and sliding down the stair railing, his left clutching the documents to his side. He descended below the rotunda floor all the way to George Washington's basement crypt to escape the pandemonium above. He made it without encountering anyone who might be able to finger him as a witness. As he headed for the gallery, he was almost trampled by a team of white-smocked medics from the Capitol physician's office running full speed the other way, toward Stu's wrecked body.

Once safely back in the gallery he closed the door to his booth, plugged the thumb drive into his computer, and began to read and listen.

It was all there. Phone records and account statements. An audio file of Dickey's voice making calls and plotting, not only with Stu, but with dozens of people all over town. There was sound of the majority leader conspiring to defraud the market and fatten up his campaign coffers with dirty money, in the process ripping off thousands of ordinary Americans who held Minton stock. And that was on top of a conspiracy to bankrupt the company with false rumors of financial irregularities.

It was devastating and it was damning. Taken together, the computer drive and the documents from Stu amounted to the biggest blockbuster story Tom could have hoped for.

After it all sank in, Tom had an idea.

# Chapter 30

The ABN producers called Dickey's office and explained to a bewildered receptionist that they were running a Tom Salta piece about how the majority leader planned to force his own daughter into a sham marriage with his closest aide in order to keep her from marrying another woman, a woman who happened to be Representative Polk. The aide had killed himself instead, just moments after handing Salta the whole story.

Dickey's staff in the Capitol were paralyzed with fear. Despite Dickey's power and reach in Washington, the press shop was a mom-and-pop operation that might as well have been run out of an old cigar box. On a good day no one but Dickey and Stu knew anything. Now Stu was dead, Dickey had gone to ground, and the office was in rampant chaos. Aides were inundated with thousands of e-mails, calls, Tweets and Instagram, Snapchats, and Facebook postings, all focused on Dickeygate. Cable TV reporter live shots

streamed from cell phones outside in the hall. The office was under siege. There was no push-back because no one dared step up.

The producers said the story would lead the news under the
banner, "Sex, Lies, and Suicide: Dickey Exposed." The entire
first block of the broadcast would be devoted to the sordid tale—
an unprecedented level of coverage, exclusive to ABN News.
And so the producers wanted to know this of Dickey: in the
name of fairness and balance, would the leader be prepared to
give the network a statement?

At home, Dickey was in a panic but had one more card to
play. He would call the Minton CEO—the selfsame individual
whose company and career Dickey was trying to destroy. As he
picked up the phone, he got a rare glimpse at the outskirts of
shame. It was an apparition that vanished as quickly as it appeared. This was no time to be proud.

It was Tom Salta and Congresswoman Polk on that filthy
tape that had been broadcast on Senate TV!" Dickey angrily
shouted into the phone. Unless Tom was fired at that moment
and his story spiked, he vowed to call a press conference in five
minutes and tell the world what a disgrace to journalism ABN
and its reporters represented. Most importantly, he would release
the full, unpixelated video shot of Tom Salta and a certain member of Congress in their full glory. They'd be all over YouTube,
in flagrante delicto.

"I do not get involved in news reporting decisions," the Minton CEO said haughtily in response to Dickey's tirade. He mentally calculated the number of times ABN was about to be mentioned around the world over the next twenty-four hours, weighed that positive against the damage to the brand, and decided he stood a reasonably good chance of having it both ways: ABN would have the pride of ownership for being the one to break the story of Dickey's unbelievable venality, and then jump on a high horse about journalistic ethics in time to fire this guy Salta.

He had spent the better part of his day in crisis mode, fighting renewed rumors of an impending congressional investigation of Minton for malfeasance, mismanagement, and insider trading. The stock was taking yet another beating. He suspected Dickey, of course. But he was only partially to blame. Turns out the whole thing started when this idiot, Salta, had pitched it as a story on a conference call where hundreds of people with their life savings wrapped up in Minton stock were listening. The first thing that happened was that half of them went online to shift their money to a mutual fund, while the other half called their contacts on the Street to find out what they knew. It might as well have been tweeted out by the Wall Street Journal. A mini panic ensued. What it all came down to in the end was the elemental hatred the CEO harbored for that fucker Zach Dickey, a bedrock truth that made everything a lot easier. Once the story aired, he would be rid of both him and Salta, a guy who obviously didn't have the sense to know where his own bread got buttered.

"I suggest you call Steve Sunshine, the president of our news division," said the CEO to Dickey. "Good-bye, Mr. Leader." Dickey could be heard screaming through the thin air of the seventy-second floor of ABN headquarters as the phone traced its arc from ear to cradle.

Sunshine was on the other side of the spacious office, gripping a five iron and practicing his form. "News is about to get a call from that son of a bitch Zach Dickey," the CEO said. "Ignore him."

Sunshine halted at the top of his backswing, careful to keep his left arm straight and club shaft properly positioned parallel to the floor.

"Done and done," replied the newsman, starting his downward move, the club head whooshing through the hitting zone. He stood posing as he envisioned a perfect power fade, carrying the bunker and landing softly 250 yards down the lush fairway of his mind.

Back in the sputtering heart of his rapidly failing political machine, Dickey had gone on for at least thirty more seconds of histrionics before realizing that the phone was dead and his bluff had been called. Now there was no choice. Well, there was technically a choice. He could pack it in, claim demonic possession in the form of booze, avarice, ambition, or a combination of deadly sins, book it to rehab, and then publicly emerge to seek redemption and reunion with his Lord and forgiveness from the rest.

But that would all take too long, and he had big ambitions. He was going to have to get out front, starting with busting out Salta and Loretta. He hesitated, evidence of at least one shred of decency left. Going public would mean exposing his daughter's sexuality. But that was likely to happen anyway. So he applied another Dickey axiom, which over the years had become a catchphrase, a kind of totem for loyal staff past and present, invoked in crises large and small. It went like this: "Moral distinctions can paralyze you."

He said it so much it had become a meme in Dickey world, serving as a kind of secret handshake among staff and favored lobbyists. A choice between a home-state colleague who had been a friend for years and a young up-and-comer who raised lots of campaign money for a seat on Ways and Means? Whether to appear at a fundraiser, thrown for your benefit, hosted by a Tennessee company currently under investigation for illegally dumping contaminants into the Sequatchie River? Threatening to cut off pork projects to a loyal lieutenant's district if he didn't change his vote on campaign finance reform? All deliberation concluded the moment Dickey declared, "Moral distinctions can paralyze you." As long as the alternative wasn't clearly illegal, it really wasn't much of a choice. He would take the low road. Hurt feelings would heal. Good soldiers are useful, but good soldiers die first.

# Chapter 31

Washington weather, like its politics, is a zero-sum game. Damp, bone-chilling cold in the winter or damp, suffocating heat in the summer. No in-betweens and misery either way. The gauzy shroud that settles over the town is briefly lifted in May and again in October, an ephemeral reminder of the limitless universe beyond the soupy muck.

The Saturday after Tom's report aired was one such day. The morning broke in a pale green light, the oozing humidity drawn away to its Bermuda redoubt. Soon the city would awaken to the first rime frost, providing the citizens of the capital their subliminal cue to let go of summer fantasies and get back to the careerism and ambition that defined their lives.

Zach Dickey awoke in a fit of choking. The monoxide miasma of a dozen satellite trucks seeped into his home. He was a man besieged, a prisoner with no one to turn to but his wife, who for the last few years had been merely a semirecluse with a drinking problem, but who was now a certified lush who never got out of her bathrobe. His plainclothes police detail, usually ready and eager to talk women and sports, sat apart playing cards on the backyard deck. They clearly wanted to be somewhere else. The constant rumble of the media encampment—generators with their pounding hum and microwave towers extending and retracting—rattled the family china in the dining-room breakfront.

Stu was dead. His daughter, his beloved Cornelia, his only child, was estranged and not likely to ever speak to him again. She was to be married to Loretta that very day. His political allies in the national party were not returning his calls. Members of Congress who two days ago feared and respected him, who would have done anything to gain his favor, had made themselves scarce. All throughout the nightmare of yesterday not one had dared break through the cordon of reporters staking him out to offer a word of encouragement or support. Not one. Literally overnight his face had become an international symbol of corruption and worse, the agent of financial ruin for millions of companies and individuals around the world.

It was Dickey's personal Armageddon in two acts. First was the tale of how the last firewall of filial loyalty crumbled when he had the colossal nerve to try to force his daughter, Cornelia, and Stu Albertson, his loyal and long-suffering aide-de-camp, into a sham marriage. And why? Because his daughter was in love with a woman. And not just any woman. None other than

Representative Loretta Jean Polk, the alluring widow and rising political star. A political dynasty torn asunder. An epic celebrity scandal. Tom's report on ABN.com had ten million hits in the twelve hours after its debut on the evening news show.

Act two was all about Minton and Dickey's vengeful plot to bring it down, including audio of Dickey himself conspiring to slander the company with false rumors of financial irregularities. All part of his plan to defraud the market and fatten up his campaign coffers with his ill-gotten gains, in the process stripping hundreds of thousands of ordinary Americans of their life savings. It was devastating and it was damning.

But that story didn't air on ABN. That distinction went to CNB, Gil Jorgenson reporting. That was the inspiration that came to Tom after he had digested what Stu had handed him: to give Gil the real substance, the information and the elements for the story that would make and break fortunes. It was much more than a gesture of affection. It was a thanks for setting an example of what journalism should be, a tribute from Tom to Gil's integrity, and an admission by Tom that he wasn't worthy to carry Gil's notepad. More importantly, it was a story that would force a shake-up of vital national institutions that for years had corroded from within. Tom knew it would be in good hands when he gave it to Gil.

The repercussions were already rippling through markets and beyond, with experts across platforms talking about bursting bubbles and trade imbalances and all the weakness in the world economy laid bare by the diabolical folly of one man, the hated American politician Zach Dickey.

The situation at the Dickey residence was approaching hysteria. Media swarmed from Chile, South Africa, Singapore, Japan. There were five networks from China alone. For years Dickey had pandered to the xenophobes and nativists by proudly stating that he had never set foot outside the United States and never intended to. "All anyone could ever need is right here in America." A fail-safe applause line. But now the globe was at his doorstep. Sounds that to his ear couldn't possibly constitute a coherent language were emanating from the mouths of reporters holding microphones and talking into the cold glass of a camera lens. The time differences between Washington and their home country meant someone was bound to be jabbering around the clock, TV lights illuminating the scene like an Alaskan solstice. Dickey's quiet residential Washington lane was now a cultural milieu. He hadn't slept in two days.

They were everywhere: not just his Capitol office and his DC home, but his place back in Tennessee, where he himself hadn't been for months. They were at his daughter's house, Stu's house, the airports. There would be no escape. Not without a Princess Di–style paparazzi chase. The only thing left for him to do was to hole up and wait it out. For the first time in his life Zach Dickey felt sorry for himself.

BOP aired the details of Tom's role in the saga, starting with the disclosure that it was in fact Tom and Loretta Jean Polk in the now legendary piece of video that aired for but a brief few seconds on CON-NET but now lived in perpetuity on the World Wide Web. BOP reported a tale of how an unscrupulous and callow reporter attempted to entrap a beautiful and dedicated public servant by blackmailing her for information on Zach Dickey. In BOP's version, Salta, desperate to redeem himself after having been scooped repeatedly the preceding week by the veteran BOP news team, was there on the night the video was shot to accompany Representative Polk to a charity masquerade ball at nearby Union Station. Salta presented himself at her door with his face hidden behind a bio-hazard mask, explaining to the congresswoman that the theme of his costume was space travel to alien civilizations. But once inside Polk's office, Salta slipped a dose of a known aphrodisiac into the mineral water of an unsuspecting Polk. The unfortunate result was an emotionally and morally broken American icon whose descent into iniquity was witnessed by millions. Lewdness that was an affront to common decency. The report concluded with the reminder that the video could now be seen exclusively and in its entirety on BOP.com. Dickey had given Billy the raw tape, following through on this threat. But instead of changing the subject as Dickey had hoped, the video put the whole saga into the troposphere. The audience was insatiable.

A media maelstrom roared. It was the mother of all clusterfucks, with more stakeouts at Loretta's, at the ABN bureau downtown, and at Tom's place over in Chevy Chase. The cables were apeshit, with plans for staying on the air all weekend, even those that were normally in prerecorded infomercials by midafternoon. All kinds of tidbits were being unearthed about the principals, dating back to youthful pranks gone awry or brief hallway encounters that were now extrapolated and distorted by analysts eager to demonstrate their unique insight. They preened and pontificated, wrung their hands and clutched their pearls, all the while letting it be known that they had suspected all along that it would end this way. Among the revelations delivered with a note of solemn indignation: Salta had been suspended from high school for sending mash notes to his eleventh-grade Spanish teacher ("clearly portentous") or that Loretta was frequently seen at Mistrial, a noted lesbian hangout tucked away in a downtown alley ("we would normally not traffic in this kind of innuendo"), or that Dickey used his connections to get his daughter a position at Minton ("sadly, the kind of influence peddling that gives Washington a bad name"). Cornelia was savaged as a vapid harlot, a parasite living off her father's reputation. And it was only just beginning.

# CHAPTER 32

"**M**an, you have got to get off your ass!" It was Dana on the line, and he was disgusted. "Do something, for shit's sake! This is not the Zach Dickey that I knew in 'Nam."

"I don't think there's any use, Bugsy," Dickey told his old friend. He had just set the scene—the cameras, the stakeouts, the calls for his head. The likelihood of an investigation by the FBI's Public Integrity Section, and probably the SEC. "Hell, from the looks of things outside my fence gate, the United Nations might empanel a commission. Or just haul me up at The Hague. The way this is going I might be the next Milosevic," said Dickey, pronouncing the Serbian war criminal's name so it sounded like a popular antacid. "I'm lyin' here trying to figure a way out of all this, but it just ain't comin' to me. This might be the end of the road for ol' Zach Dickey," he told Dana. "And I'll just tell you straight up, Bugsy. I don't even care about the rest of it. What with losing Cornelia this way, I don't believe I give a damn what happens to me. It's breaking my heart, is what it's doing."

"That fucking turf muncher!" Dana spewed.

"Oh, now that is uncalled for!" Dickey shot up off the couch. She may have been that very morning committing an unspeakable sin—and just to think of it was another punch to the gut—but she was still his daughter. "I will not stand for anyone to speak of Cornelia in that manner! Not even you!"

"Whoa now, Zach. You know that I would never do such a thing." Dickey had always been a man of action and conviction, and if it were possible to be someone's equal in friendship while at the same time hold them in awe, well, such was the nature of Dana's feeling toward Zach Dickey. The country needed him. Bugsy needed him. That's why he had to get Dickey back on his feet and making moves. "I wasn't talking about Cornelia, Zach. Heavens no," he continued. "It's that two-faced Loretta Jean Polk. She's behind all of it. We all fell for her song and dance. At least, I know I did. And we both know that Cornelia is no kinda lesbian."

"That's the damn truth right there, Bugsy," Dickey said. But he had no fight in him. "I believe that age has finally taken its toll," he sighed. "When you're young, the tide in the harbor is always high. But then you get old and the tide rolls out, and the wrecks at the bottom are all exposed."

"But sometimes you find a lost treasure," replied his friend. "You can't give up!"

"I appreciate what you're saying, old friend," said Dickey. "But I reckon what's happening today has been a long time coming."

"If Cornelia had never fallen in with that Loretta, that fucking tramp—pardon my French—none of this would be happening right now. You'd still be planning to run for president. And hell, if there were any justice in this world, you *would* be our next president."

"Damn her!" cried Dickey into the receiver. "Damn that wicked creature!"

Dickey's ranting could be heard through the speaker of Dana's phone, disturbing Dana's wife, who sat riveted before their living room television. "Dana, please. The language? I can't hear what they're saying on the TV," she said from the edge of the sofa.

"Turn that goddamn thing off!" Bugsy screamed. Then he looked at what his wife was watching on the television screen and had a revelation. "Zach, are you seeing this?"

"Watching what? TV? I couldn't bear it, no."

"Zach, turn on BOP right now. I want you to see this, and then I want to ask you a question."

Dickey did as his friend asked and hit the power button on his remote. At first he could hardly make out what was happening. "Breaking News" graphics, "Live" on-screen bugs, and drop-line chyrons cluttered and stretched the images. The live BOP camera was being jostled by others as they all maneuvered to get a shot of activity on what appeared to be Main Street in a small town. The shot switched to an aerial view branded "BOP Force One." The camera panned over acres of hilly pastureland until it held a shot of a white-steepled chapel in the center of a country village, in front of which a great many people had gathered, certainly more people than could have resided in such a tiny place. The on-screen bug reported the location as Paris, Virginia, out in the foothills past Dulles. Then the drop line changed, and before Dickey could make out what it said, the house was filled with a shriek that no human could have heard and not had a vision of hell itself.

Dickey wheeled around to see his wife, stirred from last night's drug- and alcohol-induced stupor by her husband's rant. She had a hank of hair in each hand and was pulling as hard as she could. Next came a sound originating beyond the boundaries of conscious thought, as she cried out as if a six-quart pan of boiling water had been poured over her shoulders. Her eyes held such terror that for a moment Dickey didn't recognize his own wife in his own house. He followed her stricken gaze across the room to the television, and at that moment he understood what brought on her outburst.

"Polk and Dickey Daughter to Arrive at wedding ceremony within the Hour; Plan to Wed," read the chyron on the TV screen. It was all really happening. Their Cornelia was marrying Loretta Jean Polk that very day.

Dickey had to steady himself. "Where is this place?" he asked Bugsy through clenched teeth.

"About thirty miles west, in the Blue Ridge. Which brings me to the question I wanted to ask you."

"The answer is yes," Dickey said. "The only thing I want you to tell me is how."

The lion-hearted warrior Dana had known those many years ago in a distant war would not sit idly by and suffer this unspeakable insult to the Dickey family name. It wasn't right, what was happening to him. Now Dickey had awoken. He would fight!

"Well, sir, can you fly a Bell 430?" Bugsy asked.

Dickey had flown choppers for hours every day in Vietnam, in and out of combat zones and on countless rescue missions, or ferrying brass all over the Mekong Delta. Yet he had not been at the stick in quite some time. Twenty years, maybe. He was definitely out of practice. What's more, he in fact had never been at the controls of a 430.

"Hell yes!" he said decisively.

"Good. I'll make a few calls. This thing is supposed to happen around noon. That's two hours. Plenty of time, if you get going right this second."

"Where?" Dickey asked.

"Old Line Airport. A little strip over on Route 50 east of town. The local ABN affiliate keeps their traffic chopper there. They know me at the airport. I've shot video out the side of that thing a million times. It won't be a problem."

"Thirty minutes," Dickey barked. He hadn't felt a rush like this since back in 'Nam. Zach Dickey was back in the saddle. His blood was up.

"I'll meet you there," said Dana.

His police detail heard the chirp of the SUV's remote and the sound of doors unlocking, but by the time they ran into the alley, Dickey was already behind the wheel with the engine running. The only thing left to do for the people who were supposed to be protecting him was to get the hell out of his way before he ran them down. Dickey hit the gas and the behemoth roared down the alley.

Two camera techs were lounging nearby in fold-up campaign chairs, one's face in the sports page and the other's a John Grisham novel. They looked up just in time to save themselves from destruction, yet could only watch helplessly as Dickey plowed through a thicket of tripods and light stands, accelerating as $80,000 cameras bounced off the SUV's grill. His tires squealed as he turned into the asphalt and sped away.

"Holy shit! Was that Dickey?" someone shouted.

"It was Dickey!" one of the now-gearless cameramen confirmed.

"*Ikimashita!*" exclaimed a Japanese correspondent.

There was a pause as a wave of comprehension swept over the scrum. Then, as if on cue, the mob rose as one and started for their cars, frantically punching numbers into cell phones as they ran. Dickey had the jump on them. He was a quarter mile away before the first car jammed with producers, reporters, and camera crews piled in and sped off in his wake.

He was already on the Southeast Freeway before he saw the first media car coming up fast from behind him in his rearview, a tech with a camera on his shoulder standing up through the sunroof. A small flotilla of Crown Vics and Tahoes wasn't far behind. Dickey hit the siren and punched the gas. Cars in front of him slowed and pulled out of his lane, leaving a clear path as he pushed forward ever faster. But the horde pursued. Young production assistants held their phones aloft outside car windows, trying to live stream the chase at eighty miles per hour. By the time they hit Kenilworth Avenue, it was a scene from *Mad Max*, with media cars pulling up alongside trying to get a clear camera shot. They knew it would be the only video of the chase…all of DC inside the Beltway had been declared a no fly zone after September 11, including news choppers. No aerial video. This could be their only chance, and it was essential that they get the shot. They were all doing ninety by now.

Dickey lost them at the exit for Route 50. He zigged left, passed a car in the middle lane, then zagged right at the last minute, slaloming around a terrified senior at the wheel, and holding his middle finger aloft for the cameras as he zoomed down the ramp and east toward Old Line Airport.

# CHAPTER 33

The glossy black helicopter sat crouched in the airfield like a panther, "News Chopper 13" emblazoned in big yellow letters on its side. Dickey figured it could probably do close to 190 at a decent altitude. He peered into the cockpit and saw doodads all over the control panel that looked like they were probably important, quite possibly vital. He had no idea what they were for.

*Like riding a bike,* thought Dickey. *It don't matter if it's got one speed and a basket on the handlebars or it's something you see in the Tour de France. You never forget how.*

Dana drove up, jumped out of his car without bothering to close the door behind him, and ran to meet Dickey. The two men climbed into the chopper and Dickey started the rotor. His feet seemed to know what to do on their own, and the two men and their machine were off the ground just as media cars, kicking up dust and gravel, screeched to a halt at the edge of the runway.

Bugsy leaned out of the airborne chopper and yelled down at his awestruck colleagues.

"Eat shit and die, scum!"

A young reporter for ABN's local affiliate was on the phone. "Uh, boss," he stammered, "you're not going to believe this, but I think Zach Dickey just stole our chopper."

At that moment the news director was watching a live stream of the scene on a cell phone held before his face by a young production assistant. He saw, but his eyes did not believe. "What the hell do you mean?" the news director bellowed.

"Well, I just saw him and that old cameraman Bugsy fly off down Route 50, heading west. Bugsy just flipped us all off from about three hundred feet up."

To the news director, who lived in a perpetual state of aggravation—a side effect of his metastasizing technophobia—this information made absolutely no sense and therefore made perfect sense. "That chopper cannot be flown! The goddamn transponder is out!" he shouted. "Why do you think it's sitting there at a moment like this when every fucking thing that can fly is out in the Blue Ridge at the wedding?"

The helicopter gained speed and altitude. Already Bugsy and Dickey could see the Capitol dome ahead in the distance, with the Washington Monument a mile farther on and the Lincoln Memorial another mile beyond that, and a few clicks later, the Blue Ridge Mountains. All in a straight line running east to west. The easiest thing to do would be to follow the course they set until the mountains came into view—visual flight rules—then start looking for all the aircraft hovering like flies over a mound of dog shit. That's where he'd find this so-called wedding. And his Cornelia.

Dickey had neither the time nor the inclination to try to figure out all the dials arrayed before him. All he needed to know was how fast and how high, and that was plain enough on a day like today. They didn't bother with comms. They knew what they would hear if they did: all kinds of people ordering or begging them to land. That wasn't going to happen. Anyway, this wouldn't take long. They'd be there in no time. Dickey knew what he had to do, and there wasn't a damn thing that was going to stop him.

Of course, with the radio down, they couldn't hear the hysterical calls from the ABN newsroom warning them of a broken transponder. Nor could they hear the repeated calls from Air Traffic Control to identify themselves and their flight plan. There was no way to know who they were or what their intention was. They were merely an unidentified blip on the radar screen, airborne and flying directly toward the hallowed symbols of American freedom and democracy.

# CHAPTER 34

To a girl from Wyoming, the mountains of the east hardly merit the name. They're older than the Rockies, that is true. And it's said that once upon a time much of the Appalachian chain stood even taller and mightier than The Grand Tetons themselves. Yet over millennia the elements had worn their peaks and crags down until they were, in the present age, little more than large, rounded, grass and tree covered humps.

No, they were not colossal, as mountains go. Yet their size did not diminish their status, for to stand among them was to feel small. Their ancient dignity lent a perspective that induced a feeling of tranquility, much as one gets from staring at a wildfire, or the eternal cycle of ocean waves. To bear witness to the timeless immensity of nature was to understand how insignificant our worries, our striving, and our very lives, really were. For a couple that had been through as much as Loretta and Cornelia, a country inn nestled in the foothills of the Blue Ridge was the perfect setting for a wedding.

"Love is our best friend, our helper, and the healer of the ills that prevent us from being happy," began the Unitarian minister. Loretta and Cornelia stood before her, straining to hear the words of their own ceremony over the thumping of helicopter blades echoing in the hollows, and the whirling whine of tiny video drones buzzing just overhead.

It was a beautiful day, and despite the intrusion from above it was a lovely event, both poignant and pretty. The wedding party, small though it was, had entered one by one to a soaring trumpet voluntary. They walked atop a white paper runner that had been unspooled along their path, past bouquets of red roses lashed with purple ribbon to the end of each row of white folding lawn chairs. There was Scotty, the bouncer from Fester's, all smiles as he walked up the aisle. Loretta and Cornelia each had someone from childhood there, their roots of friendship deep enough to withstand the storm of controversy surrounding the day. Two of Loretta's staffers were in the procession. Paul, the purple-headed page, bore the rings on a satin pillow, bringing up the rear.

The trumpet quieted, and a harpist began to play Pachelbel's Canon in D as the two women started their walk up the aisle. Instead of one playing the part of groom and waiting for the other at the altar, the pair had bucked tradition and decided to walk together. It wasn't intended as any sort of statement. Rather, they were simply making a virtue of necessity. Neither woman wanted their father anywhere near them on their wedding day.

The guests sat scattered among the rows, beneath strings of sea glass glittering in the sunshine overhead. There was to be a reception after the ceremony, and the inn's staff looked on, standing at a respectful distance but close enough to be able to later claim they were there at the center of the media universe that day. In all, there were about thirty people seated, or roughly a quarter as many guests as there were reporters standing on the street outside the property line. The guests were mostly friendly Hill staffers, along with a random cousin here or there. The CEO of Minton Systems sat in the second row, beaming as if his own daughter were up there tying the knot.

"To understand the power of love, we must understand that our original human nature was not like it is now, but different," the minister read from Plato's origin myth of human sexuality. "There were three sexes then: one comprised of two men called the children of the Sun, one made of two women called the children of the Earth, and third made of a man and woman called the children of the Moon," the minister went on.

"The Gods feared the power and might of these humans, so Zeus divided the humans in half. Each of us, when separated, having one side only, is but the indenture of a person, and we are always looking for our other half. Those who come from the children of the Earth are women who love other women. When one of us meets our other half, we are lost in amazement of love and friendship and intimacy, and would not be out of the other's sight, even for a moment."

Loretta and Cornelia exchanged vows, and then each took a ring from Paul and slipped it on the other's finger as they declared their love.

The minister was bringing the ceremony to a close. "Remember that your future lies in the path you have chosen together. Enter into marriage knowing that the true magic of love is not to avoid changes, but to navigate them successfully.

"You may now kiss your spouse." The pair came together in a passionate embrace. The guests stood and applauded.

At that moment the inn's sommelier, who had been stealing glances at something on his cell phone all throughout the ceremony, screamed at the top of his lungs. Everyone turned to look at the man.

The next thing the wedding party heard was a distant rumble, like rolling thunder.

# Chapter 35

The two F-16s out of Langley had been killing time at twenty thousand feet, flying long, languid loops on their routine Civil Air Patrol around the city. It was a mission that had been flown virtually without incident everyday since 9/11.

The urgent order was to get down to one thousand feet, make visual contact with an unidentified helicopter that was entering restricted air space, arm the Sidewinders and AMRAAMs, and engage. With the chopper's course, speed, and heading, there would be no time to try to get out in front or next to it, no wagging the wings or gesturing from the cockpit before the aircraft entered the no-fly zone over Washington that had been in place since that horrible day of the September 11 attacks.

The pilot in one of the F-16s locked onto the chopper and fired, scoring a direct hit.

The helicopter became a fireball, its molten debris scattering from the east front of the Capitol to the west, showering tourists and joggers alike with searing fragments of fuselage, engine, and rotor. Five people on the ground were killed instantly; another twenty-seven would end up in trauma centers around the city with severe burns and missing limbs. Adding to the devastation, one missile missed the target and scored a direct hit on the dome of the Capitol, puncturing the cast iron of both inner and outer shells and igniting a fire in the rotunda that incinerated everyone and everything inside. The intense heat melted a gilded copy of the Magna Carta into a formless blob. When the smoke cleared, the pock marked and mangled dome looked like something out of Mogadishu, a ruinous consequence of anarchy and civil war. Inside, it was simply a charred ruin.

Majority Leader Zach Dickey and his friend Dana Siegel were vaporized in an instant, their spectacular destruction seen live around the world. Taken in the aggregate, the countless hours of video shot on cell phones provided gruesome images of the carnage from every conceivable perspective. The scenes of horror would be witnessed by tens of millions in a matter of minutes.

That night the networks would extend their normal half-hour broadcasts to a full hour. But that was half a day after the cataclysmic events, and by that time most people had seen enough, or at least they didn't need an evening news program to show them what was at their fingertips whenever they wanted to see it.

The billions of page views generated on the web outnumbered the total TV audience worldwide by a factor of a thousand, both in terms of total viewers and within the coveted twenty-five to fifty-four year old demographic.

# EPILOGUE

*"The only security of all is in a free press."*

—*Thomas Jefferson to Lafayette, 1823*

The First Lady was nervous. After spending much of the campaign trying to stay out of sight, this would be her first major public appearance. And it wasn't just some silly bit of ceremonial puffery, like unveiling holiday decorations in the Blue Room. This was an on-camera appearance before the elite of American life, who, along with a viewing audience of millions, would be watching her every move as she took her place on the dais.

The occasion was the White House Correspondents Dinner, an unsavory confluence of the national news media with the world of entertainment. The affair was an annual orgy of self-reverence, featuring the inexplicable fawning over Hollywood celebrities by Washington journalists. The machinery of media, politics, and pop culture, well lubricated by three days of garden parties and corporate events, meshed and mixed until you could almost see the conventional wisdom congeal in real time over cocktails and canapés. On the big night of the dinner, the crowd was about one-third movie stars, one-third news reporters, and one-third lobbyists and executives from the companies that owned the networks. It was the apotheosis of American power. The keynote moment would come when all present stood as one in the vast hotel ballroom to raise a glass and toast the ultimate celebrity, President Loretta Jean Polk.

"Why do we have to do this?" Cornelia asked, reaching for Loretta's hand as they awaited their introduction. Two years had passed since that fateful day of soulful joy and then, moments later, unimaginable catastrophe. Over that time the arc of their lives had shot over the moon and back.

The shards of burning iron from the wrecked Capitol dome had not yet cooled before the interview requests and offers for Loretta and Cornelia began to pour in. Booking the big "get" was always blood sport among competing news networks. First, they deployed their biggest stars to beg the newlyweds for a joint appearance. The ante soon escalated to a one-hour prime time special devoted to the couple and the story of the romance that shook the world. Finally, ABN took the bidding to its logical extreme, offering Loretta her own spot on the network grid. Primetime and a guaranteed twenty million dollars a year for five years.

The pitch was for Loretta to host a sort of political reality show. Ordinary citizens with dreams of political power could come to an open audition and be allotted three minutes to make a speech. From that number, a dozen with promising polemical chops would be chosen to compete. Cameras would follow an aspiring candidate/contestant from speech to speech, fundraiser to fundraiser. Along the way Loretta would coach them up, offering pointers on how to improve their rhetoric and schmoozing skills. The video would then be edited down to a two minute tape, which would in turn be reviewed and graded by a panel of experts, chaired, of course, by Loretta. The three top finishers would be invited to make a final appeal for support live on the two-hour season finale in front of the panel and a few hundred members of a studio audience, who would have the chance to vote for their favorite. The winner would receive a half million-dollar campaign contribution.

The show was a runaway hit.

Loretta's rise to fame and popularity were meteoric, and the next step was an inevitable and forgone conclusion. In less than a year's time she vaulted to the top of every pundit's list of likely presidential candidates and was polling far ahead of the nearest competitor. She was immune to scandal, inoculated by the prevailing narrative of how as a congresswoman she had been victimized by the media and corrupt party leaders. When it came to Loretta, the threshold for shock and indignation had already been raised so high that no scandal or dirt could ever tarnish her brand, much to the frustration of her opponents. She joined the race for president, forming a new, third political party, and ran on a platform of free love and free enterprise. She was elected in a landslide.

As President Polk and First Lady Cornelia Polk prepared to take the stage in Washington, a dad in a Nags Head, North Carolina, skate park sat on a bench, keeping an eye on his young kids grinding and carving their way around the ramps and rails. Every once in a while he glanced down at the tablet in his lap, where he was streaming the White House dinner live on CON-NET. The dad was all about Loretta Jean Polk, and he didn't want to miss a moment. He had gone to his local polling place on Election Day, showing up to vote for the first time in at least five cycles. His long years of negligence meant he was no longer on the active voter rolls, so the election judges made him fill out a provisional ballot, which in all likelihood wasn't going to be counted when all was said and done. He didn't care. He was crazy about Loretta Jean Polk, to the point where he had packed his whole family into the car in the pre-dawn hours of Inauguration Day and drove the six hours to Washington, just to catch a glimpse of Loretta being sworn in. They could barely make her out from their spot behind the acres of reserved seating, but he would have moved heaven and earth just for the chance to say he was there.

"And now the White House reporters will welcome President Loretta Jean Polk, accompanied by first lady Cornelia Polk, " reported Gil Jorgenson, the off-camera anchor of CON-NET's broadcast of the dinner. After his report on CNB outlining the financial scandal around Dickey and Minton Systems, Gil was offered a retirement buyout package, which he took. Now he split his time between CON-NET, where he hosted viewer call-in shows, and a part-time gig at a Rockville, Maryland community college, where he taught a class in journalism.

The Marine Band struck up the first notes of "Hail to the Chief," as the skate park dad watched with mounting excitement, He turned up the volume as his hero Loretta Jean walked on stage with Cornelia, and the whoops and cheers from the adoring DC ballroom crowd could be heard through the tablet's speakers, drowning out the music.

Tom Salta grew agitated as he stood behind the counter of the skate park. "Sir, would you mind turning that down?" he asked the man.

Tom had rushed to Capitol Hill in the moments after Dickey met his spectacular doom. Swept away in a of melee if panic, he found himself side by side with Janine the Dream, the bartender from "Corinthian's," when they became trapped together in the chaos behind police lines. Together they witnessed what seemed to both of them a vision of the Apocalypse. The Capitol was on fire, and sirens rang out in every direction. Despite the fact that Dickey's chopper had been blown out of the sky on live video seen by millions, there were wild rumors of terrorism: that bad guys had detonated a bomb in the Rotunda; that the entire National Mall was aflame; that the president had been shot. The police commanders were improvising, and their only consistent and coherent orders were to push the public as far back from carnage as possible. People screamed and sobbed as they ran.

As he huddled with Janine among the bewildered and panicked masses, Tom had an epiphany: *I am done.*

No more of the empty ambition that had marked his time in Washington. Life was too short. Turning to Janine, he proposed they run away and get married. Elope, the old fashioned way. They would chuck it all, go some place warm with a beach and start some sort of mom-and-pop operation, living their lives in shorts and sandals, answering to no one but each other.

Janine said yes. A month later they moved to the beach and bought a skate park. Tom named it, "Stu's."

Just after Loretta's victory in the presidential race, Tom's old talent agent tracked him down one day in Nags Head. He was there to relay an offer from ABN executives, who wanted to know if Tom would come back to the network as the chief White House correspondent and cover the incoming Polk administration. They told the agent to tell Tom they wanted an experienced hand at the helm in such a critical time.

By that time Janine was pregnant with their first child. The skate park was doing well enough to allow them to live a life of low pressure and plenty of beach time. Tom was happy. He was married to a beautiful and loving woman, and she was happy, too. They were building a life and a business together. Tom almost fell over with laughter when he heard the pitch.

Clearly, despite everything that had happened the network bosses couldn't resist the idea of Tom sitting in the front row of a presidential press conference, grilling his partner in history's most famous sex tape on the big issues of the day. Three years ago an offer to leave the congressional TV gallery for the White House pressroom would have been a dream come true for Tom. Now he couldn't have imagined anything he would rather do less. He bought his old agent lunch, then sent him on his way back to New York with the bad news for his old bosses.

That life, that era, that way of thinking, was over.

THE END

# Acknowledgements

M uch of this book was written in the early 2000's, and then put away in the proverbial desk drawer until recently. Given all the time that has passed, it may be virtually impossible for me to thank all of the people who have encouraged and inspired me along the way. But I'll try. Special thanks to Dale Stein, Dominic Ambrosi, Karl Ackerman, Matt Dolan, Larry Schultz, Jason & Sabrina Wallach, and Kim Viqueira for volunteering their time to read the manuscript and make suggestions.

Thanks to Jim Mills, Ted Barrett, and Dean Norland for memories that will last a lifetime.

And thanks to the 'Lids, true friends to the end.